MONTANA BRIDES

Welcome to Montana—a place of passion and adventure, where there is a charming little town with some big secrets…

Storm Hunter: He'd returned home to set the record straight about big brother Raven. But he'd fight to end his growing attraction for a very young lady—with Kincaid blood running through her veins—innocent beauty Jasmine.

Jasmine Kincaid Monroe: What Jasmine hated most was being considered a baby. Her mother, Celeste, coddled her, and now the magnificent Storm Hunter refused to see her as more than a girl. Well, Jasmine would turn virgin seductress to tame Storm. But would she be able to hold on to him?

Celeste Kincaid Monroe: Her recurring nightmares were hidden memories seeking salvation.

Lyle Brooks: His funeral lent closure to one recent death, but what secrets lay buried with him?

Dear Reader,

Welcome to the wonderful world of Special Edition!

This month we're continuing Muriel Jensen's immensely popular WHO'S THE DADDY? series with *Daddy in Demand* which we've chosen as our THAT'S MY BABY! story.

Renowned author Laurie Paige gives us the second intense instalment of the WINDRAVEN LEGACY with *When I See Your Face*. While Gina Wilkins kicks off her brand-new HOT OFF THE PRESS trilogy with *The Stranger in Room 205*—an amnesia tale with a striking twist.

Meanwhile, Christine Scott brings us *Storming Whitehorn* which is the last of the four MONTANA BRIDES books. Plus, a modern fairytale comes from Barbara McMahon in *Starting with a Kiss*, and then there's a rugged loner wondering if he's husband and father material in *Stranger in a Small Town* by Ann Roth.

Enjoy!

The Editors

Storming Whitehorn

CHRISTINE SCOTT

SILHOUETTE®
SPECIAL EDITION™

*First published in Great Britain 2002
Silhouette Books, Eton House, 18-24 Paradise Road,
Richmond, Surrey TW9 1SR*

© Harlequin Books S.A. 2000

*Special thanks and acknowledgement are given to Christine Scott
for her contribution to the Montana Brides series.*

ISBN 0 373 65061 2

23-0702

*Printed and bound in Spain
by Litografia Rosés S.A., Barcelona*

CHRISTINE SCOTT

says, 'Since I was a kid, I've either been reading books or trying to write them. Growing up at our house, bedtime was strictly enforced—lights out at eight o'clock. But that didn't stop me from sneaking the flashlight under the covers and reading until the early hours of the morning.'

'It wasn't until I found my real-life hero, married him and had our three children that I gave serious thought to writing a romance. Four years ago I finally got that first call from an editor at Silhouette, telling me they wanted to buy my book. For me, it was a dream come true. Now, eight books later, I'm still hooked on romances.'

Christine Scott grew up in Illinois, but currently lives in St Louis, Missouri. A former teacher, she now writes full-time. In between car pools, baseball games and dance lessons, Christine always finds time to pick up a good book and read about…love. She loves to hear from her readers. Write to her at Box 283, Grover, MO 63040-0283, USA.

If you enjoyed

MONTANA BRIDES

you'll love to know that it's not over yet...

April 2002
The Marriage Maker   by Christie Ridgway

May 2002
And the Winner—Weds!   by Robin Wells

June 2002
Just Pretending   by Myrna Mackenzie

July 2002
Storming Whitehorn   by Christine Scott

**The latest Montana Brides
four-book series coming
to you from Silhouette
Special Edition®**

MONTANA BRIDES
THE KINCAIDS

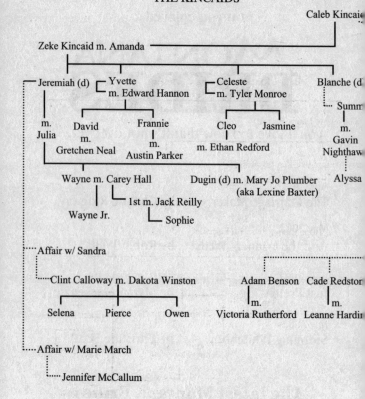

Caleb Kincaid

Zeke Kincaid m. Amanda

Jeremiah (d) — Yvette
m. Edward Hannon

Celeste
m. Tyler Monroe

Blanche (d

Summ

m.

Julia

David
m.
Gretchen Neal

Frannie

m.
Austin Parker

Cleo

m. Ethan Redford

Jasmine

m.

Gavin
Nighthaw

Wayne m. Carey Hall

Dugin (d) m. Mary Jo Plumber
(aka Lexine Baxter)

Alyssa

Wayne Jr.

1st m. Jack Reilly

Sophie

Affair w/ Sandra

Clint Calloway m. Dakota Winston

Adam Benson   Cade Redstor

Selena   Pierce   Owen

m.
Victoria Rutherford

m.
Leanne Hardir

Affair w/ Marie March

Jennifer McCallum

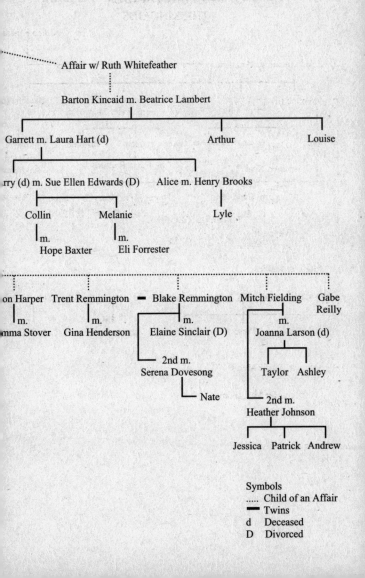

Affair w/ Ruth Whitefeather

Barton Kincaid m. Beatrice Lambert

Garrett m. Laura Hart (d)   Arthur   Louise

...rry (d) m. Sue Ellen Edwards (D)   Alice m. Henry Brooks

Collin   Melanie   Lyle

m.   m.
Hope Baxter   Eli Forrester

...on Harper   Trent Remmington   ▬ Blake Remmington   Mitch Fielding   Gabe
                                                                        Reilly
m.   m.   m.   m.
...mma Stover   Gina Henderson   Elaine Sinclair (D)   Joanna Larson (d)

                              2nd m.   Taylor   Ashley
                              Serena Dovesong

                                      Nate   2nd m.
                                                     Heather Johnson

                                              Jessica   Patrick   Andrew

Symbols
..... Child of an Affair
▬ Twins
d   Deceased
D   Divorced

To Bill, a great brother and a cowboy at heart.

One

"She's never been this late before." Jasmine Kincaid Monroe crossed her arms at her waist and stared out the large front window of the Big Sky Bed & Breakfast.

Jasmine's aunt, Yvette Hannon, joined her at the window. A tall, striking woman with classic features and graying hair, she exuded an enviable grace and confidence. Her smile reassuring, she placed a warm hand on Jasmine's slender shoulder. "Knowing your mother, she probably bumped into an old friend in town and has lost all track of time. I'm sure Celeste is all right."

"My mother hasn't been all right in a long time. Not since—" Jasmine stopped, frowning as she averted her gaze.

"Not since they found Raven Hunter's remains," Yvette finished with a sigh.

Raven Hunter was a name from the past, which had only recently resurfaced with a vengeance. Thirty years ago, Raven and Jasmine's aunt, Blanche Kincaid, had been illicit lovers. When it had been discovered that Blanche was pregnant, their affair had caused a scandal in the Kincaid family, as well as in the town of Whitehorn. Blanche's brother, Jeremiah, had vehemently opposed any suggestion of his sister marrying a member of the Cheyenne. It hadn't been long after Blanche's pregnancy was revealed that Raven disappeared. Some say Jeremiah had paid him off, that Raven had taken what money he could get and run. Others say he'd loved Blanche too much, that he wouldn't have abandoned her. They believed Raven was dead, most likely at the hand of Jeremiah Kincaid.

Apparently, the latter was true.

For, at the construction site of the new casino/resort that straddled the Laughing Horse Reservation and the Kincaid ranch, Raven's remains had been recently uncovered. A bullet lodged in the rib cage confirmed Raven had died a violent death. The discovery set into motion a chain of events that had led to two more deaths, the most recent of which had hit too close to home. Jasmine's family was still reeling with the news of their cousin Lyle Brooks's death.

"This investigation into Raven Hunter's murder is wearing on Mother. Why won't she talk to us? If she'd just tell us what's wrong..." Jasmine let the words drift into a frustrated silence.

Choosing her words carefully, Yvette said, "Darling, you have to understand what this must mean to your mother. I was at school in Bozeman when Raven disappeared, but Celeste was still there at the ranch.

Despite Jeremiah's opposition, she stood by Blanche during her pregnancy and when she gave birth to your cousin, Summer. She was also with Blanche when she died. It was a very trying time for everyone, but most of the burden fell on Celeste. Discovering Raven's body has dredged up a lot of painful memories. Is it any wonder that your mother might be upset?''

''No, I suppose not. But she isn't sleeping, Aunt Yvette. I hear her up at night, pacing. Last night, at two o'clock in the morning, I found her sitting cross-legged on the floor in the middle of her bedroom, surrounded by candles, burning incense and chanting.'' She shook her head at the thought. ''When she turns to the spiritual world, there has to be something more than just memories troubling her.''

''She was chanting?'' Yvette's brow furrowed. ''Celeste does have a strong belief in the spiritual hereafter. Perhaps she was calling upon the spirits to help Raven find peace at last.''

''It isn't Raven Hunter who needs to find peace, it's my mother,'' Jasmine said, her voice sharper than she'd intended. She sighed. ''I'm sorry, Aunt Yvette. I didn't mean to snap.''

''It's all right, dear,'' she said gently. ''I know you're worried.''

Absently, Jasmine touched the gold-plated compass hanging by a chain around her neck, and felt her heart catch with emotion. The compass had been a gift from her mother when she'd turned twenty-one and had returned home after finishing her training at the culinary school. Because of Jasmine's love for hiking in the mountains, Celeste had told her it was her reassurance that Jasmine would always find her way home.

With the memory strengthening her resolve, Jasmine strode to the front desk and snagged her purse from behind the counter. "She should have been home hours ago. I'm not waiting any longer. I'm going to Whitehorn to look for her."

Yvette followed her to the desk. "Perhaps you're right. I'll take care of things here at the B and B while you're gone. You will call, won't you? If you find anything…anything at all."

At the sound of her troubled voice, Jasmine squeezed Yvette's arm. "I'll call."

Releasing her aunt, Jasmine strode to the front door. The heels of her cowboy boots tapped against the lobby's pinewood floor, matching the nervous beat of her heart. She wiped a clammy hand down the length of her short pleated skirt. Despite late August's cooling temperatures, she felt hot and sticky. Her eyelet shirt clung uncomfortably to the curves of her body. Pushing aside her discomfort, she stepped outside onto the large, open porch that ran the length of the front of the house.

By the time she reached the first step of the wooden stairs, however, she noticed a cloud of dust being kicked up on the lane that led into town. Jasmine stopped, squinting at the rapidly approaching car. From what she could see, the luxury car was a silvery gray, one that she didn't recognize. An unexpected guest for the B and B, she supposed. With an impatient scowl, she reminded herself that she didn't have time to greet a visitor. Yvette would have to handle this new arrival.

Gravel crunched beneath its tires as the car slid to a quick stop in front of the manor house. Coughing, Jasmine waved a hand in a vain attempt to clear the air of the dust whipped up by the skid. A fine layer of grit floated over her like a powdery blanket. Once the dust settled, the driver's door opened and a tall, dark, handsome Native American man stepped out onto the driveway.

He was muscular, with broad shoulders and narrow hips. His hair was straight and black, with touches of gray at the temples. He wore it long, to the collar of his buttoned-down shirt, and all one length. Lifting his sunglasses from the bridge of his nose, his dark brown eyes glimmered in the sunlight as he fastened a gaze upon her.

Jasmine froze, unable to move as he slowly raked his eyes up and down the length of her body. Never before had she been subjected to such a blatantly assessing stare. She nearly trembled beneath its weight. It felt as though he were undressing her with his gaze.

Despite the differences in their ages—his she guessed to be late thirties, or early forties; hers a mere twenty-three—she felt an instant stirring of awareness deep in the pit of her belly. A sensual heat warmed her blood. She was surprised by her strong reaction to this total stranger, but not intimidated by him. Instead, she returned his stare with a curious gaze of her own.

The stranger was the first to break the spell that seemed to hold them both. His deep voice rumbled in her ears as he asked, "Is this the Big Sky Bed & Breakfast?"

"Y-yes, it is," she said, stumbling over an assent. Rolling her eyes at her clumsiness, she cleared her throat and began again. "I'm Jasmine...Jasmine Monroe. My family owns the B and B. May I help you?"

"My name's Storm Hunter," he said, his eyes never leaving her face, as though testing for her reaction. He stepped toward her, closing the distance between them. "And I believe that I'm the one who can help you."

Hunter? Jasmine's heart skipped a beat at the name. Storm Hunter, Raven Hunter's brother. She'd heard he was back in town. Her cousin David Hannon, a special agent for the FBI who'd been on a leave of absence since shortly after the remains of Raven Hunter had been found, had mentioned Storm's tempestuous arrival in Whitehorn. The two men had nearly come to blows when Storm had refused to accept the lack of progress in the investigation of his brother's murder. Apparently he bore a personal grudge against anyone with a connection to the Kincaid family.

Goodness only knew why this forceful man was now standing on the driveway of her family's bed-and-breakfast.

"I don't understand," she said, unable to hide the skepticism from her voice. "*You* want to help *me?*"

A corner of his mouth lifted in a semblance of a polite smile. "Perhaps I should clarify. What I meant was, I believe I have something that belongs to you." With a sweep of his hand, he gestured toward the front seat of his car.

For the first time Jasmine noticed another person inside. There, slumped against the passenger door, was Celeste Monroe, Jasmine's mother.

"Mother!" Jasmine gasped in alarm. She turned, calling over her shoulder for her aunt's support. "Aunt Yvette, come quick. It's Mother."

Not bothering to wait for her aunt, she pushed past the disturbing Storm Hunter and hurried to her mother's side. Wrenching open the car door, she was stunned by her mother's pallid complexion. Her short, russet hair looked disheveled. A fine layer of perspiration dampened her skin.

Gravel crunched beneath his shoes as Storm joined her. She glanced up at him, her gaze accusing. "What have you done to her?"

He flinched at her bitter words. A reaction that he

quickly hid behind a stony mask of indifference. His expression cool, he said, "I haven't done a thing to your mother. She fainted at the sheriff's office in Whitehorn. I was there when it happened. I offered to drive her home. She accepted. That's the extent of my involvement."

Jasmine's face grew hot with embarrassment as she realized how unjust her accusation must have sounded. "I'm sorry, I didn't mean to—"

The skin around his finely sculpted cheekbones grew taut. His jaw stiffened, his strong chin lifting in defiance. "There's no need to apologize, Ms. Monroe. I assure you, I'm used to the white man thinking the worst of me merely because of the color of my skin."

Jasmine felt as though she'd been struck by the words. "The color of your skin? Don't be ridiculous. I never—"

"Jasmine…" Celeste's fragile voice interrupted.

Forgetting all else, Jasmine leaned forward, reaching for her mother's hand. "Mother, are you all right?"

"Take me inside," she whispered.

"Of course," Jasmine murmured.

"Jasmine?" Yvette's breathless voice caught her attention. Her aunt's cheeks were flushed from hurrying. Worry lines creased her careworn face. "What's happened? What's wrong with Celeste?"

"She fainted in town," Jasmine said quickly. She glanced at Storm. "Mr. Hunter brought her home."

"Mr. Hunter?" Yvette's troubled gaze traveled to Storm.

"Yes, *Storm* Hunter. Mr. Hunter, this is my aunt, Yvette Hannon. I believe you've already met her son, David?"

The reminder of his and David's ill-fated meeting, the one that had nearly ended in a fistfight, was uncalled for. But so was his accusation that she would judge another man by the color of his skin. When she saw Storm's eyes narrow in irritation, she couldn't help but feel a bittersweet sense of satisfaction.

Now they were even.

Gracious as always, Yvette extended a hand in greeting. "Thank you for your help, Mr. Hunter. It's, uh, good to finally meet you."

If Storm seemed surprised by this show of cordiality, he didn't show it. Instead he accepted Yvette's proffered hand with a smooth smile. "You're welcome, Mrs. Hannon. I hope your sister will soon feel better."

"Celeste, right." Yvette gave a quick nod, as though gathering herself to take control of the situation. "Jasmine, help me please. Let's get your mother inside."

Together, the two of them half lifted Celeste from the car. Celeste's white cotton, Gypsy-style shirt had come untucked from the waistband of her long broomstick skirt. The gauzy fabric sagged against her shapely curves. As was her mother's habit, somewhere along the way, she'd kicked off her sandals and was barefoot. Jasmine plucked the wayward shoes from the floor of the front seat to carry inside.

Flanking her mother on both sides, Yvette and Jasmine each held her by one arm. Slowly the three women headed for the front porch. As they neared the top step, Jasmine turned, glancing over her shoulder at the quiet figure still standing beside the silver car. "Mr. Hunter," she said, "if you wouldn't mind waiting, there's something I'd like to tell you."

Not bothering to wait for his answer, Jasmine turned away and led her mother inside.

Storm Hunter didn't like being told what to do. Not by anyone. But most especially not by an outspoken young woman who was nearly half his age.

A part of him wanted to get into his rented car and leave this place, this home of the Kincaid family, and never look back. The other part, the impulsive, illogical part, was curious as to what Jasmine might have to say.

"Jasmine," he murmured her name out loud, savoring the sound of it as it tripped over his tongue. An exotic name for an exotic beauty, he mused silently as he stood beneath the glaring sun on the white rock-covered driveway of the B and B, with his hands on his hips, staring at the door through which she had disappeared. Her image was as fresh in his mind as though she were still present.

Jasmine the woman, he decided, was a contradiction in terms. A delicate flower, as her name might suggest, though one who'd found roots and strength in the wild, untamed lands of Montana. With her black hair cut short in a pixie style, she seemed so young and innocent. The cut and color emphasized the paleness of her skin, the smooth perfection of her complexion and the classic lines of her features. Yet, at the same time, he saw the wisdom of an older woman in her eyes, one who'd experienced much of life. She was tall and slender, but with enough womanly curves to make any man stand up and take notice. Her eccentric way of dressing—black cowboy boots, a red pleated skirt and a white eyelet blouse—certainly made him wonder. Yet, the outfit hinted at a personality that was free-spirited and vivacious. Traits that he envied. Traits that he'd lost over the years, somewhere along the way.

Storm blew out an irritated breath. What was wrong with him? He was spending entirely too much time speculating about a young woman who was destined to play nothing more than a fleeting role in his life. She was a Kincaid. He was a Hunter. As history had already proven, the two did not mix. If it hadn't been for her mother and his misguided sense of chivalry, their paths would never have crossed.

Earlier, when he'd stopped by the sheriff's office on yet another fruitless call upon the investigator in charge of his brother's murder case, he'd happened to bump into Celeste Monroe. To say her reaction to his appearance had been strong would be an understatement. One fearful look at his face and the woman had collapsed in a dead faint. She'd looked as though she'd seen a ghost.

It wasn't until after she'd reluctantly accepted his offer of a ride home that he'd realized who Celeste Monroe really was. Celeste *Kincaid* Monroe, sister to Blanche and Jeremiah Kincaid, the very people he'd blamed all these years for the loss of his brother. The family who'd been at the very heart of his troubled life.

And now he was being unwise enough to let his hormones blur his judgment. He'd allowed himself to become intrigued by a Kincaid—a family he'd sworn to hate. Jasmine…

Though she'd never invited him inside, curiosity got the better of him. Quietly, Storm crossed the gravel driveway and climbed the steps of the large front porch. The double doors stood wide open, allowing anyone to enter.

Even an unwanted Cheyenne, he told himself, allowing his rancor to fester.

The floors were of polished pine. The rooms were large and spacious. The ceilings were high, measuring at least ten feet; rough-hewn beams graced the dining room ceiling. Natural wood trim stretched as far as the eye could see. The house itself was mostly furnished with the clean lines of the mission-style decor, but there were enough chaise longues and overstuffed club chairs to make a guest comfortable.

Storm stepped through one of the living room's set of French doors and onto a wide screened-in porch. The porch ran the length of the back of the house. From here, the view of Blue Mirror Lake was spectacular. Its flat, shiny surface, indeed, looked like polished glass. A dense forest of pine trees surrounded the property, and the air was thick with their pungent scent. In the distance, he saw the mountains of the Laughing Horse Reservation.

His breath caught painfully at the sight. Though he'd traveled many miles to escape from his past on the reservation, he could never completely leave behind its harsh memories. He glanced around the bed-and-breakfast, at the casual display of Kincaid wealth, and felt a bitter taste rise in his throat. No matter how many college degrees he might acquire, or how much money he made in his law practice in New Mexico, he would never forget his troubled past, his poor, hand-to-mouth upbringing. He would never be able to stand tall in a world that included the Kincaid family.

With the ghosts of the past chasing him, Storm whirled away from the sight of the reservation and strode back into the house. The heels of his shoes pounded against the pine floor as he made his way to the front door. But he didn't care about the noise. He didn't care about anything but escaping.

"Mr. Hunter…Storm." There was a note of desperation in Jasmine's sweet melodic voice.

Storm clenched his jaw in annoyance and told himself to keep walking. Don't look back. Don't stop, no matter how great the temptation might be.

Her boots tapped an urgent beat against the wood floor as she hurried toward him. Guiltily, he heard the breathless quality of her voice as she called, "Please wait. I'd like to talk to you."

A heavy hand of frustration pressed against his shoulders, slowing his pace. Though he was only a few steps from a clean getaway, he couldn't find the strength to abandon her. He chided himself for being so weak-willed and wondered what it was about this woman that, when she was near, made him lose all sense of judgment.

Wheeling to face her, he didn't bother to hide his annoyance. "Ms. Monroe, I'm very busy. I don't have time—"

"This won't take long," she assured him. Her cheeks were flushed from exertion. Her chest rose as she took in a steadying breath. "I—I just wanted to thank you."

He raised a brow in disbelief. "*You* want to thank *me?*"

She nodded. "That, and to apologize."

He didn't respond. Instead he waited for her to continue, purposefully schooling his face to be void of expression, uncertain whether to trust her unexpected change of heart.

"Earlier I jumped to the wrong conclusion. When you brought my mother home, she looked so weak and helpless, I—I was shocked. I said the first thing that popped into my mind. I accused you of hurting her, without knowing the facts. For that I'm truly sorry. Please don't think that I would judge you, or anyone else, for that matter, solely on the color of their skin. Because it just isn't true."

He believed her.

During her plea for understanding, Jasmine had looked him straight in the eye. Her gaze had never wavered, not once. Either she was the coolest liar he'd ever met, or she was telling the truth.

He'd bet the house on the latter.

Grudgingly he asked, "Your mother, is she all right?"

"She's fine," she said, striving for a lighthearted tone, and failed. Blushing, she gave a self-deprecating smile and added, "Or at least she will be, now that she's home. Thank you, once again, for taking care of her."

Then, with the impetuousness of the young, she reached out and enfolded him in an innocent hug of gratitude.

While he told himself the gesture was probably not unusual for this woman who seemed so open with her own feelings, he wasn't prepared for such a free-spirited reaction. To his chagrin, his body reacted in a most uncordial manner.

With her soft curves pressed against him, he felt himself harden in response. His hands caught her waist with the intention of pushing her away. Instead he found himself pulling her closer.

As though she sensed a shift in the mood, Jasmine pulled back. With her hands still linked behind his neck, she lifted her eyes to his. A slight frown wrinkled her brow. Her look was not one of alarm, but rather of curiosity.

Her face was turned upward to his. Her lips, so soft and full and inviting, proved too much of a temptation. Once again, he lost his battle with willpower.

Knowing full well all the reasons why he shouldn't be doing this, Storm was unable to stop himself. Slowly, his eyes never leaving her face, he lowered his head and brushed his lips against hers.

He heard the quick inhalation of her breath, felt the rise and fall of her breasts against his chest, and waited for her to resist. But she didn't. Instead she leaned forward, tilted her head in a more accommodating position and silently encouraged him to deepen the kiss.

Logic and reason escaping him, he brushed his tongue against her lips and felt them open to him. Gently he explored the moist heat of her mouth, savoring its sweet taste.

Closing her eyes, she collapsed against him, letting

her softness mold his body. She clung to him, burying her fingers in the hair at the back of his neck, bringing a delicious shiver coursing down his spine.

A low moan of desire escaped his throat as he tightened his grip on her waist and let the kiss deepen. Storm had never felt this way before, this recklessness, this intense yearning for more. Proof was in the fire in his belly, as well as in his heart. This was different. Jasmine was different. After a lifetime of loneliness, it had taken him only a moment to realize what had been missing.

She was the one.

He had finally found his soul mate.

The unexpected thought came from out of nowhere, chilling him. Abruptly he ended the kiss. Winded, he sucked in deep drafts of air as he stared down at her flushed face. Her lips were swollen from his caress, and her eyes sparkled with an excitement that he had ignited. He felt another surge of desire for this woman deep in his loins.

He tore his gaze from her face and forced himself to look at the pale, white arm that rested against his own coppery skin. Once again, the differences in their lives came crashing down upon him, screaming out to him what a fool he'd been.

Jasmine Kincaid Monroe would never be his soul mate. The only thing they shared was a star-crossed history. What he felt for her was lust, plain and simple.

As his brother before him, he wanted what he could not have. The sooner he realized that, the better.

With the harsh reminder echoing in his mind, he pushed himself from the tempting warmth of her embrace and turned away. He hurried outside. Rocks crunched beneath his shoes as he strode to the car. He slung himself into the front seat, gunned the engine to life and shifted the car into gear. Gravel and dust spewed from beneath the tires as he spun out onto the driveway.

Midway down the lane into town, he allowed himself to glance into the rearview mirror. Like a dream that had disappeared upon waking, Jasmine was no longer there.

Two

Jasmine felt numb the next morning as she stared across the rolling green slopes of the Whitehorn Cemetery. The sky was overcast, the sun hidden behind a bank of storm clouds, making the white marble headstones and the simple limestone crosses appear almost luminescent in the false twilight. A cool breeze swept the grounds, carrying with it the promise of the long winter ahead. She shivered in her simple black dress, wishing she'd remembered to bring a sweater.

Moodily, she blamed her lack of forethought on Storm Hunter. Him, and his damned kiss. Since yesterday she'd been unable to think of little else. Thoughts of Storm and their encounter had left her restless and preoccupied. He'd come and gone in a blink of an eye like a fast-moving tornado, but the damage he'd left behind had been devastating.

Her womanly pride had been shattered.

Pushing the troubling thought from her mind, she concentrated on the ceremony taking place. Along with a small gathering of the Kincaid clan, Jasmine had come to pay her respects to a cousin she barely knew. For this was the day that Lyle Brooks was being laid to rest.

While they'd been close in age, only a year apart, Lyle had spent most of his life in Elk Springs. It wasn't until recently that he'd made his presence known in Whitehorn. A presence that had spelled trouble from the start.

Though the details were still sketchy, Lyle's fateful business dealings had rocked the small town of Whitehorn. He'd been a major player in the planning of the casino/resort that would encompass both the Kincaid property and the Laughing Horse Reservation. His grandfather, Garrett Kincaid, had entrusted him to oversee the family interest in the project. A decision that an obviously distraught Garrett now regretted.

For reasons unknown, Lyle had killed one of the construction workers at the building site by pushing him off of a forty-five-foot ledge. When Gretchen Neal, the lead detective on the case, uncovered his culpability in the crime, Lyle had tried to kill her to silence her. Before he could carry out his plan, Jasmine's cousin, David Hannon, had shot and killed him in a gun battle.

Construction on the new casino/resort had been halted, its future in limbo. The business deal, which would have been profitable for both the town of Whitehorn as well as the members of the Laughing

Horse Reservation, had been dealt a lethal blow. One from which no one was certain it would recover.

Now they were gathered here to pay their respects to a man who hardly deserved them. Even before they'd discovered the extent of Lyle's evil, Jasmine had never felt comfortable around her cousin. He'd had such a dark aura, and there were always too many bad vibrations emanating from him.

Jasmine frowned. Dark aura? Bad vibrations? Good grief, she was starting to sound like her mother. She sighed. Mystical nonsense, or not, Lyle Brooks was one man whose spirit she wanted to see settled, not roaming free to cause more heartache.

She scanned the group, looking for familiar faces. Her mother and her sister, Cleo, were nearby. As well as Aunt Yvette and Uncle Edward, with their daughter, Frannie, and her husband Austin, at their side. Noticeably absent, however, was their son, David, the man responsible for Lyle's death, and his fiancée, Gretchen Neal, whom he intended to marry come spring.

Garrett Kincaid, with his distinctive head of silver hair, stood tall and straight at the front of the group, supporting his grief-stricken daughter, Alice Brooks, Lyle's mother. Alice's husband, Henry, hovered at his wife's side, helplessly patting her arm, trying to ease her sorrow. Henry looked pale and hollow-eyed, devastated by the loss of his only son.

Across the way, Jasmine spotted her cousin, Summer Kincaid Nighthawk. When Summer's mother, Blanche Kincaid, had died, Yvette and Celeste had taken her under their wing, raising her as their own daughter. Inseparable since childhood, Jasmine and Summer were like sisters. Now, though Summer wore a somber expression and her long dark hair was gathered into a severe bun at the back of her head, Summer glowed with an internal happiness that couldn't be dimmed even in the darkness that surrounded this day. Obviously marriage to Gavin Nighthawk agreed with her.

Some of the new cousins were in attendance also. These were the illegitimate sons of Larry Kincaid, Garrett's only son, who'd recently been united on the Kincaid ranch. While Jasmine barely knew this new batch of relatives, it felt good to have them gathered around her. It gave her hope for a new beginning, the possibility of a familial closeness yet to come.

The minister's final blessing rose above the cry of the wind and Alice Brooks's sobs of grief, signaling an end to the service. With a nod toward Garrett, the minister picked up a handful of newly spaded dirt and tossed it onto the bronze casket as it was lowered into the ground. In turn, Garrett and Henry Brooks followed suit, letting a fistful of dirt sift through each of their hands.

When it was Alice Brooks's turn to perform the ritual, she stood beside the gravesite, shaking uncontrollably. Then, with an ear-piercing scream of anguish, she threw herself onto the casket, wailing inconsolably. The winches holding the coffin shuddered at the added weight. The groundskeeper operating the lift fumbled with the switch, cutting the power. A communal gasp of surprise arose from the crowd.

"For God's sake, Alice. What are you doing?" Garrett called, reaching for his daughter.

At first Henry Brooks stood frozen to the spot, his eyes wide, his mouth dropping open in surprise. At the sound of his father-in-law's gruff voice, he gave a visible shake, ridding himself of his stupor. Quickly he grabbed for his wife.

Alice clung to the casket, stubbornly refusing to relinquish her death grip. Jasmine's heart went out to the woman. Though Alice had a reputation for being shrewish, no one deserved to suffer such grief. After a few agonizingly discomfitting moments, the two men finally coaxed her to loosen her hold. They pulled her away, half carrying, half leading her from the gravesite.

The crowd dispersed amid murmurs of shock at the dramatic scene they had just witnessed.

Shaken by the unexpected events, Jasmine turned to leave. As she did so, she spotted a tall figure at the fringe of the gathering. He stood apart from the group, almost hidden beneath the shading branches of one of the many pine trees that stood sentry over the hallowed grounds. But she had no trouble recognizing him.

It was Storm Hunter.

Her heart skipped a beat as she stopped and stared at him, wondering why he'd come. Though he saw her, he didn't move, nor did he look away. Instead he held her gaze without flinching.

In deference to the day's event, he wore a black, double-breasted suit. His starched-white shirt complemented the darkness of his skin. His long hair was slicked back *GQ*-style, emphasizing his high cheekbones and the sculpted line of his jaw. Despite his grim expression, he looked breath-stealingly handsome.

Memories of the kiss they'd shared flooded her mind, warming her skin with a sensual flush of heat. She could still feel the pressure of his mouth against hers, could still taste his lips. Desire still pulsed through her body.

Though her pride had taken a blow when he'd left her without a word of explanation, she found herself drawn to him like a willow branch to water. She stepped toward him, her mouth curving into a tentative smile of greeting.

But the cold, prohibitive look in his eyes stopped her. Jasmine stumbled to a halt, shivering beneath his frosty glare. Holding her gaze for just a moment longer, he turned away, spurning her once again.

She couldn't move, couldn't think what to do next. An unfamiliar chill of rejection enveloped her, stiffening her limbs, numbing her mind. Never before had she been rebuffed by a man twice in as many days. The experience was as humiliating as it was crushing to her ego.

Until now she'd thought of herself as a desirable woman. At least, the men in town had certainly made her feel that way. She'd never wanted for a date, not since she'd turned a sweet sixteen. But with all their clumsy attempts to woo her, none of the local men had ever come close to arousing in her the earth-shattering sensations she'd experienced with Storm's single kiss. What made his rejection even harder to understand was that she could have sworn Storm had felt the same way.

"Jasmine?" Summer's soft voice interrupted her pensive thoughts. She linked arms, pulling Jasmine close to her side. "You're trembling. Are you all right?"

Jasmine watched Storm's departure through the cemetery while trying to focus on her cousin's words. "It's just the wind, the cold. I'm fine, really."

Summer frowned. "You don't look fine. You look as though you've lost your best friend."

No, just a chance at something wonderful.

Summer followed the direction of her distracted gaze, her frown deepening. "Do you know that man?"

Jasmine bit her lip, hesitating before answering, uncertain what to say. Storm Hunter was Summer's uncle. Though Storm had left Whitehorn long before her birth, and had never bothered to contact her since, he was still her closest living relative on her father's side. She wasn't sure what Summer's reaction might be to his appearance.

Unable to lie to her cousin, Jasmine said, ''That man was Storm Hunter, your uncle.''

Summer flinched at the words. Her gaze startled, she looked across the cemetery grounds to the chapel's parking lot where Storm was climbing into his car. Pain and confusion filled her eyes. And Jasmine realized she wasn't the only woman feeling rejected.

Jasmine muttered an oath beneath her breath. Damn the man. Since arriving in Whitehorn, Storm Hunter had caused nothing but trouble for every single person his presence had touched.

Hadn't he done enough damage?

For her sake, as well as her family's, perhaps it would be best if he returned to where he'd come.

One hand clenching the steering wheel, Storm put the cemetery far behind him. With his free hand, he loosened his tie and wrenched it from the collar of his shirt. Fumbling blindly with the top button, he breathed a sigh of relief as it popped open. A suit and tie were his daily lawyer's uniform, but today the outfit felt as though it were choking him.

At least, that was the excuse he allowed himself for his agitated state. He refused to blame his foul mood on his reaction to seeing Jasmine again. He told himself that the white-hot flash of desire he'd felt had nothing to do with his quick departure from the cemetery. Nor did it have anything to do with the lingering conviction that somehow he and Jasmine were fated to be together. No, he wasn't running away. He'd merely accomplished what he'd set out to do— see for himself the family that had destroyed his life. The Kincaids.

Only, until he saw her standing alone amid the mourners, he'd forgotten that one of the Kincaids included a member of his own family. Summer Kincaid, his brother's only child.

Storm drove slowly through Whitehorn's downtown area, passing the police station and the movie theater. Down the street from the courthouse, he spotted the Hip Hop Café. Though it was too early for lunch, he didn't think he could face the four silent walls of his hotel room. He needed a place where he could go to unwind and not have to listen to the sound of his own guilty conscience.

He pulled into a space and parked the car. Tossing his suit coat into the back seat, he headed inside the café. A country tune by Garth Brooks greeted him at the door. A handful of patrons were scattered around the café, some at the counter, others in booths. Heads turned at his entrance. Curious glances followed him as he made his way to a booth in the back. Whether they were staring at him because he was a Native

American or because he was overdressed for the lunchtime crowd, he wasn't sure.

Since arriving in Whitehorn, he hadn't felt an open hostility from any of its residents. Though he couldn't say he felt welcomed, either. Bigotry was alive and well across the country. Whitehorn was no worse or no better than any other town. No matter how much he'd like for it to be different, he would never be able to convert everyone to a world of complete acceptance.

A waitress with a bright smile and long blond hair pulled back into a ponytail, joined him at his booth. She plunked a menu down onto the Formica-topped table and set a coffee mug next to it. Without asking, she filled his cup to the brim with the steaming brew. "If you're looking for breakfast, you're half an hour too late. We've already got the grill set up for lunch."

Storm shook his head. "That's okay. Coffee's fine for now."

"Sure thing," she said with a nod. "My name's Janie. If you need anything else, just holler."

Storm watched as Janie made her way to the front counter. His mind drifted back to the haunting scene he'd witnessed at the cemetery. Other than Alice Brooks's histrionics, he had to admit the Kincaid family had seemed normal. They weren't the monsters he'd remembered them to be as a child.

For years he'd clung to his hatred of the Kincaid family like a lifeline, finding solace and strength in bitterness. He'd blamed them for Raven's unexplained disappearance, not wanting to believe that his brother would have abandoned him unless he'd felt he'd had no other choice. While Raven had talked little of his affair with Blanche Kincaid, Storm knew he'd been disturbed by Blanche's older brother, Jeremiah. Jeremiah had been the devil incarnate. He'd belittled Raven in public and had threatened him in private. There was little doubt in Storm's mind that Jeremiah Kincaid had played a role in Raven's death.

If only he could get the police to agree.

Storm picked up his mug, blew the steam off the top and took a sip of the hot coffee. Once the mystery behind his brother's death had been officially solved, he intended to be on the first plane back to Albuquerque. There was nothing here to keep him in Whitehorn.

Nothing but a family he'd turned his back on.

And a niece he did not know.

Storm set the mug back on the table. He stared at the clouds swirling across its cooling surface, as though searching for a way to soothe his guilt. In the days since he'd returned to Whitehorn, he'd seen Summer a handful of times. Always from a distance, never face-to-face.

He'd told himself he was waiting for the right moment to approach her. Only that moment had yet to come. Today he'd been just a few feet from finally meeting her. But as was too often the case, when it came to facing up to his personal responsibilities, he'd chosen the easy way out. He'd run.

Storm closed his eyes and took in a painful breath. For thirty years he'd lived with the thought that his brother had abandoned him. Wounded and betrayed, he'd purposefully distanced himself from the town and the people that had reminded him of his loss.

But now he knew the truth. Raven had died all those years ago.

Storm had run out of excuses to hide. His brother was gone for good. But Raven's daughter was still alive and well. And she was his last link to the only person he'd ever loved.

With a deep sigh, he opened his eyes. Glancing around the café, he caught the eye of the blond-haired waitress.

Smiling, she strolled over to his booth. "Did you change your mind about lunch?"

"No," he said, shaking his head. "I'd just like to pay the bill."

"That's too bad," she said, tearing a page from her receipt book and placing it on the table in front of him. "Fried chicken's the special today. The cook fixes a mean bird."

Storm gave a polite smile. "Thanks, but I'm not really hungry. Maybe you could help me with something, though. I'm looking for someone. Summer Kincaid. Do you know her? Or where I might find her?"

"Summer? Sure, I know her. She's a doctor. Your

best bet at finding her would be at the Whitehorn Memorial Hospital, or the clinic she runs at the Laughing Horse Reservation. If you can't find her at either of those two places, she's probably at home taking care of her baby stepdaughter, Alyssa. Her number's in the phone book. Only look under the name Nighthawk.'' The waitress winked as she turned to leave. ''She's a married lady now.''

Nighthawk. So Summer had married a Cheyenne. Despite being raised by the Kincaids, she'd chosen to live her life with a Native American. He felt vindicated by the thought.

He knew her name and how to reach her. Now all he needed was the courage to call her.

Slowly, Jasmine replaced the receiver in its cradle. Frowning, she stared at the phone. Summer had just called. Shortly after Lyle Brooks's funeral, she'd received an unexpected call from her uncle, Storm Hunter.

He'd asked to meet with her. Summer had agreed.

Only, Gavin was busy and unable to be with her. Summer felt the need for family support at this initial meeting with her long lost uncle and had asked Jasmine to join her.

Jasmine bit her lip. She'd do anything for her cousin, and she'd felt honored that Summer had turned to her in her time of need. As the baby of the family, Jasmine had spent most of her life being taken care of, not caring for others. She'd longed for the chance to prove herself to be mature and responsible in her family's eyes. Finally she'd been given that chance.

If only Storm Hunter wasn't a part of the picture.

She dreaded the thought of seeing him again. She didn't know how much more humiliation she could take in one day. Even if he was Summer's uncle, the man was unforgivably rude.

"Jasmine, who was on the phone?"

She looked up to see her mother approaching the front desk. This afternoon Celeste looked more like her old self. A healthy flush colored her cheeks and dressed in a tea-colored tunic and loose-fitting pants, she looked relaxed and at ease for the first time in days. Jasmine hated the idea of disrupting her fleeting moment of peace. "It was Summer," she admitted.

"Summer? Is everything all right? The baby isn't sick, is she?"

"No, nothing like that…it's just—" She stopped, struggling to find the right words. Knowing there was no easy way to break the news, she said, "Storm Hunter called. He wants to meet with her."

The healthy color drained from Celeste's face. She sat heavily on a tapestry-covered chair. "Oh, my. I knew it was only a matter of time before he'd seek her out. I suppose there's no avoiding it."

"He is her uncle," she reminded her mother.

"I know. Believe me, I know." Her hands shook

as she brushed a strand of russet hair from her face. She took in a deep, cleansing breath, in through the nose, out through the mouth. "I only wish Summer didn't have to face him alone."

"She's not," Jasmine said carefully. "I'm going over to her house now. She's asked me to be with her when he arrives."

Her mother surged to her feet. "Absolutely not. I don't want you anywhere near that man."

Jasmine blinked, stunned by the outburst. "Mother, you can't be serious."

"I'm deadly serious. The man's a Hunter. He belongs to a family that has brought us nothing but heartache. I forbid you to see him."

"You forbid me?" Jasmine's voice rose in self-righteous indignation. Since she had returned to the B and B and had taken over all of the kitchen duties, her mother had been treating her as an adult, with respect and admiration. Having Celeste now treat her like a strong-willed teenager was devastating to her ego. "Mother, I'm not a child. I'm twenty-three years old. You can't send me to my room if I don't want to do what you tell me."

"Believe me, if I thought it would do any good, I'd try," her mother said, releasing an exasperated breath. "When it comes to men, you haven't paid attention to me in years. Not since you filled out your first training bra."

Jasmine rolled her eyes. "Mother, really, would

you listen to yourself? Since when have you been distrustful? Storm may be a Hunter, but so is Summer. Are we supposed to abandon her, just because you don't approve of the other half of her family?''

Celeste took in a sharp breath, seemingly shocked by the question. ''You know I'd never abandon Summer. I've raised her since she was just a baby. I love her as much as I love you and Cleo.'' She heaved a resigned sigh. ''If Summer needs our support, then we will give it to her.''

Jasmine felt the tension ease from her muscles. Finally, she told herself, they were making progress.

The thought had no more than surfaced when her mother threw another curve at her self-esteem. With her brow furrowed into a tight frown, Celeste said, ''But that doesn't mean it has to be you, Jasmine. Surely David or Cleo could be with Summer.''

''Mother,'' she said, her tone a warning note. ''I'm going to pretend you didn't suggest that.''

Jasmine was confused and hurt by her mother's sudden lack of confidence. She didn't understand what was wrong. Normally a very liberal, open-minded person, Celeste had raised her daughters to be free-spirited and independent. It wasn't like her to be so overly protective. But then again, Celeste hadn't been acting normal since the Hunter family had resurfaced in their lives. Jasmine truly doubted that, if she were to meet anyone but Storm Hunter, her mother would care.

''Mother, I love you,'' she said, struggling to remain calm, ''and I will always respect your concern and advice. But this time you're wrong. Summer needs me. And I'm going to help her, whether you approve or not.''

Without waiting for a reply, she gave her mother a quick hug goodbye and hurried out the door. Midway to her Jeep Wrangler, her heart was still pounding and the muscles in her legs felt like jelly. She'd never felt so awful. This was the first major disagreement she'd ever had with her mother. A disagreement over a man, of all things.

But not just any man, she told herself as she rested her hand on the door of her Jeep. A man whose mutual history had had such a devastating affect upon their family. Storm Hunter.

Three

"Are you sure you want to do this?" Jasmine asked. She studied the delicate lines of her cousin's pensive face as she rocked her stepdaughter, Alyssa, in her arms.

Summer didn't answer right away. Instead she glanced down at the sleeping child, her gaze softening. Jasmine envied the look of maternal pride shimmering in her dark brown eyes. Quietly Summer said, "Storm is the last of my father's family. It's time we finally met."

"Right," Jasmine said, not bothering to hide the doubtfulness from her tone. She glanced at her wristwatch for the second time in as many minutes. "If and when he shows up, that is."

Storm was late. He should have arrived thirty minutes ago. Jasmine wished she didn't have to voice the concern she knew Summer shared. That Storm had changed his mind. That he wasn't going to come, after all.

"He'll be here," Summer said, her voice firm with conviction.

Jasmine sighed. "I wish I could be as certain of

this meeting as you are. I'm not sure I'd be quite as forgiving of an uncle who'd ignored my existence for twenty-nine years.''

"I'm sure he had his reasons, Jasmine. What matters is that he's making the effort now," Summer murmured. She stood, gathering Alyssa close. "I need to put Alyssa in bed for her nap. I won't be long."

Jasmine nodded, resisting the urge to sigh again. Instead she rose to her feet and began pacing the floor. Her protective instincts billowed inside her. She swore, if Storm Hunter didn't show up after putting her cousin through all this turmoil, the man would have to answer to her.

She stopped, frowning as she reconsidered the threat. For some reason she didn't picture Storm as a man who answered to anyone, let alone an irate woman who barely stood higher than his chin.

The doorbell rang, jarring her out of her skeptical thoughts. Jasmine jumped at the sound, her stomach knotting with unwanted tension. She took in a quick breath and released it with a whoosh, trying to relieve some of her pent-up anxiety. She was being ridiculous, she chided herself. Summer was the one who should be nervous, not her.

Speaking of whom…where was Summer? Jasmine glanced down the hall and saw no sign of her cousin. Swallowing hard at the lump of trepidation that had stuck in her throat, she forced herself to move. Her hand shook as she reached for the knob. Pasting a polite smile on her face, she opened the door to greet the newcomer.

Storm's brooding scowl stopped her. With a quick glance that grazed her from head to toe, he demanded, "Where's Summer? I was expecting your cousin, not you."

Jasmine's smile faded to a grimace. Through clenched teeth, she said, "Hello to you, too, Mr. Hunter. Your presence is as pleasant as usual."

The sarcasm was lost on this stony-faced man. He half turned from the door, looking ready to escape. Given the choice, Jasmine had no doubt that he wouldn't want to find himself alone with her. If he were, he just might have to explain his own imprudent behavior. As in, why he had kissed her, then run the day before.

Swinging his gaze back to her, he said impatiently, "Is Summer here or not?"

"Yes, she's here. She's putting the baby down for a nap." Jasmine stepped away from the door, motioning for him to enter. "Won't you come in, Mr. Hunter? I'm feeling a bit of a chill in the air."

He ignored the jab. Instead he strode past her, without a second glance, leaving behind a familiar whiff of musky cologne. The scent triggered a sensory overload in Jasmine's fickle mind, setting her nerve endings on instant alert, reminding her just how good it had felt to be held close in his arms. Oblivious to her wavering thoughts, he let his gaze travel around the living room, taking in the carpet, the painted stucco walls, and the framed photos of family scattered around. Wryly, she noted that he looked everywhere, but at her.

The silence lengthened between them, the tension in the room growing thicker by the second.

Jasmine crossed her arms at her waist, sent him an impudent glance and did nothing to lessen his unease. Admittedly she took an undeniably wicked pleasure in his discomfort. Considering his own rude behavior, she told herself, Storm was one man who deserved to squirm under pressure.

Summer breezed into the room. "Jasmine, I thought I heard the doorbell. Who was—" She stopped to stare at Storm, the look in her eye one of surprised uncertainty.

Jasmine felt a new surge of protectiveness at Summer's presence. No matter how angry she might be at Storm, she refused to let her own feelings cause her cousin any awkwardness. She stumbled over an attempt to ease the situation. "Summer, this is your uncle…Storm Hunter. Storm, this is Summer."

For a long moment neither Storm nor Summer spoke. They simply looked at each other, their gazes frank and assessing. There was no denying a resemblance. They shared the same high cheekbones, the large, dark brown eyes and the sculpted features. Summer had definitely inherited her dark beauty from the Hunter side of the family.

Summer was the first to find her voice. She gave her uncle a heartwarming smile. "Welcome to my home, Storm."

He gave a genuine smile in return. The transformation was remarkable, surprising Jasmine. The grim set of his face was softened by a tenderness she had no idea he was capable of showing. Grudgingly she acknowledged that perhaps there was reason to hope a caring man lived beneath that gruff exterior, after all.

"Won't you sit down?" Summer asked, motioning in the direction of the couch.

"Yes, thank you," Storm said. He took a seat. Then, frowning, he glanced meaningfully from his niece to Jasmine.

Taking the obvious hint, sensing that it was time for the two of them to be alone, Jasmine searched her mind for an excuse. "Why don't I make us some tea?"

Summer turned a startled look her way.

Reaching out and squeezing her cousin's arm, she murmured a brief reassurance before leaving the room. "I won't be long. I'll be in the kitchen if you need me."

Summer nodded, still looking uncertain.

Jasmine lingered in the doorway. She waited long enough to see Summer take her seat next to her uncle on the couch. The smiles on both of their faces and the soft murmur of their voices eased her qualms. She had no reason to fear leaving Summer alone with Storm. He appeared as anxious as her cousin to make this initial meeting as comfortable as possible.

In the kitchen, she put the teakettle on a low heat, giving it ample time to boil. Gathering cups and saucers, she arranged a tray that would have made her mother proud. For good measure, she even threw in a plate of cookies that she'd found in the cupboard.

After several long minutes had passed, she returned to the living room to rejoin her cousin. From the expression on Summer's face, the meeting was a success. She wore a look of utter joy, and her dark eyes glimmered with unshed tears of emotion.

Even Storm appeared moved by the encounter. His intense gaze never left Summer's face. He seemed fascinated by everything she had to say. At the moment she was talking fondly of her husband, Gavin Nighthawk.

"Gavin was so disappointed that he was unable to be here today. He's anxious to meet you."

Jasmine set the tray on the coffee table and began to fill the cups with tea.

"I'd like to meet him also," Storm said, an undeniable ring of sincerity in his deep voice. "Perhaps we should arrange another meeting soon?"

"Why not tonight?" Summer suggested, her enthusiasm bubbling. "I'm sure I could find a babysitter. We can go out for dinner. Give ourselves a chance to relax and talk without worrying about

Alyssa interrupting us." A worried frown touched her brow as she glanced anxiously at Storm. "That is, unless you have other plans."

His smile was one of patient indulgence. "No, not at all. Dinner tonight sounds like a wonderful idea. I'll look forward to it."

Summer's own smile returned. She glanced at Jasmine. "And, of course, Jasmine will have to join us. Then we'll be an even four for dinner."

"D-dinner...tonight?" Jasmine stammered. She nearly dropped the teacup in surprise. Her gaze flew to Storm's stunned face. He appeared almost as pleased as she was by the unexpected invitation. Obviously he wanted her to say no. "I—I don't know, Summer."

"Jasmine, please," Summer persisted, a silent plea in her eyes. "I won't take no for an answer."

"It is late notice, Summer. I'm sure Jasmine has made other plans," Storm said, smoothly providing her with a way out.

Jasmine glanced at him sharply, wary of any sort of helpful overture on his part. His expression had shifted from one of surprise to one of complacent smugness. He looked so damned certain that she was going to refuse Summer's invitation.

If she had half a brain, that was exactly what she should do. After all, what woman in her right mind would want to spend any more time than necessary with a man who was rude, overbearing and impossible to deal with?

But no one ever said Jasmine was smart when it came to dealing with men. Instead, as was too often the case, she let her emotions override her good judgment. Before she had a chance to reconsider, she smiled brightly and blurted, "Dinner tonight? Sounds good to me. Just tell me when and where."

For that one moment in time, Jasmine decided, the vexed look on Storm's face was almost worth the misery she'd surely suffer tonight. If only she knew how she'd explain to her mother that her dinner partner was to be Storm Hunter.

Later that evening, feeling the need to vent some pent-up tension, Storm decided to walk to the restaurant. Neela's, the restaurant, was only a few blocks from his hotel room. A short distance, one that would only take minutes to accomplish. Besides, he could use the exercise. The last few days he'd spent too many hours cooped up in his hotel room on the phone, handling his law practice in New Mexico via long distance.

With the sun down, a chill had settled over the town. The cool night air felt invigorating. He breathed deeply, welcoming its mind-clearing embrace. The longer he was in Whitehorn, the more confused he seemed to become. He didn't understand what was happening to him.

Normally he was a man who prided himself on complete control of his emotions. But now, if he wasn't losing his temper at some incompetent police officer involved in his brother's murder investigation, he was mooning over a woman. One particular woman, that is. Jasmine Monroe.

She was driving him crazy. No matter how hard he tried to avoid her, she kept popping up wherever he went. If he were a superstitious man, he'd say it was fate's way of telling him they were meant to be together. An idea that, considering the troubled history their families shared, was utterly ridiculous.

Even worse, he seemed to be enjoying their chance encounters. Whenever she was near, he felt energized. She challenged him on a level that went beyond a mere physical attraction. Despite her youthfulness, she was smart, witty and totally unpredictable. No woman had ever made him feel the way she did. Whether it was trading barbs, or simply staring into her large, doelike green eyes, he looked forward to being with her.

Before he was ready, he arrived at his destination. Reluctantly, he stepped out of the night's soothing darkness and into the harsh lights of the restaurant. Neela's, as Summer had explained to him, was a cut above the Hip Hop Café. Owned and operated by a fellow Cheyenne, Neela Tallbear, it was comfortable yet classy, boasting a rough-hewn plank flooring and polished wood tables. As a French-trained chef,

Neela had made locally grown beef her specialty. The restaurant had quickly grown in popularity, often becoming crowded.

Storm, as he soon realized, was the last of his party to arrive.

Seated at the table was his niece, Summer, and a fit-looking Native American man, whom he presumed to be her husband, Gavin Nighthawk. And last, but not least, was his dinner partner for the evening, Jasmine.

Dressed in a simple, sleeveless burgundy dress that emphasized the darkness of her hair and the paleness of her skin, she took his breath away. No matter how hard he'd tried to fight it, the pull of attraction was just as strong now as it had been the first moment he'd met her.

Storm felt as though he were fighting a losing battle.

Gratefully, he hid his unease behind the polite motions of an introduction to the man who had married his niece. He studied Gavin Nighthawk as they shook hands. Gavin's grip was strong, self-assured. He wore his hair short, anglo-style. His taste in clothes was casual yet expensive. From what Summer had told him, he was a surgeon who split his time between work at the Whitehorn hospital and the clinic on Laughing Horse Reservation. While his features were that of a Cheyenne, he appeared to be a man comfortable with the white man's ways.

Frowning thoughtfully, Storm took his seat as he realized that he and Gavin Nighthawk had much in common.

As he settled himself at the table, his knees bumped against a pair of smooth, silky legs. An electrical shock of awareness traveled up his thigh. He glanced at Jasmine as she sucked in a sharp breath and shifted in her seat, her actions telling him what he already knew. She'd been the owner of those slender legs.

"Summer tells me you're a lawyer," Gavin said, unaware of the sensual undercurrents traveling between Storm and Jasmine.

"That's right, I've set up a practice in Albuquerque."

Gavin nodded. "That's quite a way from home."

Storm's muscles tensed defensively at the remark. "New Mexico is my home. I've lived there for almost thirty years."

"I meant, from your family here in Whitehorn, those still living on the Laughing Horse Reservation," Gavin said. He placed a protective hand over Summer's, his meaning clear, his expression unapologetic.

Storm hesitated before answering. Obviously he'd misjudged Gavin. His ties to life on the reservation were still strong. His loyalty to Summer, unquestionable.

He didn't blame Gavin for being protective of Summer. If the roles were reversed and someone he cared for was faced with a relative who, after almost three decades, decided he wanted to establish a new-found relationship, he'd question the man's motives, also.

Aware of Jasmine sitting next to him, her gaze curious, Storm quietly said, "I was thirteen when I left Whitehorn. At the time the reasons for going seemed compelling. There have been many times that I wished I had reconsidered my decision. But, as we all know, what is done is done. No man can change the past."

"No, but they can change the future," Gavin murmured, lacing his fingers with Summer's. "I'm curious. Why did you choose New Mexico to work, instead of Montana?"

Because New Mexico was as far as he could run away from Whitehorn without leaving the country in which he'd been born, he admitted to himself. Out loud, however, he said, "There were many more opportunities in New Mexico. I was able to put myself through school and earn my law degree. Even now I find the work in Albuquerque challenging."

"That's too bad," Gavin said with an even smile. "We could use a good lawyer here on the reservation. Jackson Hawk is the tribal attorney at Laughing Horse. Now that he's assumed the duties of tribal leader, he's having a hard time juggling both jobs."

Again, Storm hesitated. He'd heard of the tribal leader's burdensome schedule firsthand, from Jackson

Hawk himself. Jackson had been a childhood friend. Recently they'd reconnected when he'd tracked down Storm to tell him of the discovery of Raven's remains. Since his arrival in Whitehorn, Jackson had already made a play to convince Storm to return to Laughing Horse, using guilt as his tool of choice.

Now, in the presence of his last remaining family, Storm had no intention of showing any false interest in returning to a life that had caused him nothing but pain. He'd made his choice to leave the reservation many years before. He saw no reason to change his mind now.

As though sensing his growing discomfort, Summer released an impatient breath. "Gavin, please. Just because you've returned to the reservation and have accepted the ways of our people, that doesn't mean you need to pressure everyone else into doing the same." Her eyes twinkled with undisguised mischief. "Give Storm some time. Perhaps he'll change his mind on his own."

Gavin laughed, a deep hearty laugh that chased away any tension that remained between the men. "Forgive me, Storm. I've become something of a zealot, when it comes to talking about the res. Summer tells me you've done pro bono work for the Navajos in New Mexico. And that you've taken on some civil liberty cases. Tell me about them."

For the next hour, between ordering their dinners and tackling their food, Storm, Gavin and Summer embarked on a lively discussion on the right and wrong ways to help their people. A conversation that revolved totally upon the world of the Native American.

During this time, Jasmine remained noticeably silent.

Storm tried not to feel guilty. While he hadn't set out to exclude her from the conversation, he hadn't made an effort to include her, either. Though she seemed to listen with polite interest, he wondered if she felt bored, or uncomfortable. He almost wished she did.

It would reinforce what he'd known all along. That they were from two entirely different worlds. Jasmine from the privileged world of the white man. Himself from the hard, struggling life of a Native American. It wasn't surprising that they would be unable to relate to each other on an everyday basis.

Just as they'd finished ordering dessert, Gavin's pager went off. Unclipping it from his belt, he held it up to the light and glanced at the number. "It's the clinic."

Before the words were out of his mouth, Summer's pager chirped a warning beat. Frowning, she said, "The clinic's paging me, also. If they want us both, there must be an emergency." She sighed as she rose to her feet and joined her husband, looking from Storm to Jasmine for understanding. "I'm sorry for leaving so early. But we really must go."

"Don't be silly, Summer," Jasmine assured her, breaking her silence. "Of course, you have to leave."

"I enjoyed the dinner, and our discussion. I hope we'll be able to spend more time together before I return to New Mexico," Storm said, surprised to realize he'd meant the polite words. He scooted his chair back and started to rise to his feet, preparing to leave.

"Stay," Summer insisted, shooing him back to his seat. "Just because Gavin and I have to miss dessert, that doesn't mean you must, too. Finish your coffee, eat your apple pie. Enjoy yourselves. There's no need to rush off."

Slowly, Storm returned to his seat. He glanced at Jasmine, sitting next to him. If she felt uncomfortable at the prospect of being alone with him, she gave no outward sign.

Instead she focused her attention on saying goodbye to her cousin. It wasn't until they were finally alone that she turned her head to look at him. If he thought she would remain the shy, retiring woman who'd said little for the past hour, he'd been wrong. Her cool, confident gaze sent a shiver of trepidation down his spine.

Leaning an elbow on the table, her chin resting on the palm of her hand, she looked him in the eye and said, "So, tell me, Mr. Hunter, what sort of game do you think you're playing?"

"Game?" Storm sat back in his chair and studied

her carefully. "I assure you, Ms. Monroe, I don't know what you're talking about."

She raised a finely sculpted brow. "Don't you?"

Not trusting himself to answer, he raised his hands in mock surrender, feigning a confusion he did not possess. "Really, I haven't a clue."

She ran a slender finger over the rim of her water glass as she considered his response, the action catching his attention. Finally, without so much as a blink of an eye, she said, "You kissed me yesterday. An unexpected experience, yes, but special, nonetheless. Both of us seemed to have enjoyed ourselves. Since that time, however, you've been avoiding me. I'd like to know why."

Storm's breath caught at her bluntness. Taken aback, once again, by her penchant for complete honesty, he was at a loss as to how to answer. The truth was, she scared the hell out of him. The kiss they'd shared had been more than special. It had been magical. An experience he'd like to sample again and again. But he'd be damned if he was going to admit that much to her.

Buying himself time while he thought of a way out of this tenuous situation, he lifted a hand and motioned for the waitress. When the heavy, round-faced Cheyenne woman arrived at their table, he said curtly, "We're finished. I'd like the check."

The waitress blinked in surprise. "But what about

dessert? I was just about ready to bring out the pies—''

"We've changed our mind," he said, refusing to look at Jasmine for her reaction. "You can add the cost to the bill, but we won't be staying to eat them."

The waitress heaved a tired sigh and shook her head. "Yes, sir, whatever you want."

Flipping through her receipt book, she totaled up the cost of dinner and handed him the check. Without looking at the amount, Storm handed her his credit card, not wishing to delay his departure a minute longer than necessary.

Raising a brow, the waitress said, "I'll run this through the machine. Be back in a jiffy."

With that, he was alone once again with Jasmine. And he realized he could no longer avoid what must be done. Once and for all he must make it clear to her that there was no possibility of a relationship between them. There were too many obstacles standing in their way.

Whatever means he must take, it was Jasmine's turn to be scared away.

Leaning forward in his chair, keeping his tone confidential, he said, "I'd be careful what I ask for if I were you. You might not want to know the answer."

A slow smile stole across her beautiful, exotic face. "And what is that supposed to mean?"

"It means, my dear Jasmine, that you are just a child," he said, keeping his voice smooth and silky, like a caress. "And I am a man of many, many experiences. The kiss that we shared was nothing compared to the things I know to please a woman. And you, little one, are nowhere near ready to handle what I can do for you."

The smile faded. Her lips parted in a silent gasp of surprise. She looked…stunned.

Satisfied, Storm rose to his feet. Tipping his hand in mock salute, he turned and left, not daring to glance back at the woman he was leaving behind, lest he changed his mind.

Her mouth still drooping in surprise, Jasmine stared after Storm's departing figure. He moved through the crowded restaurant with the primal grace of a predator. With his wide shoulders and narrow hips, he reminded her of a sleek mountain cat, coiled and ready to spring into attack.

Suddenly the room felt as though the heat had been cranked up by at least twenty degrees. Feeling flushed, on a shaky breath, she murmured, "Oh, my."

The waitress chose that moment to return. She glanced at Storm's empty chair. "What happened to tall, dark and in-a-hurry?"

Jasmine's face warmed with embarrassment. "He had to leave."

"What am I supposed to do with his credit card?" She held up the gold card for Jasmine's inspection. Its shiny surface glittered beneath the muted lights of the restaurant.

The slow smile returned. Jasmine told herself he may be cool and collected on the outside, but Storm Hunter wasn't as in control of his emotions as he'd like for her to believe. She held out a hand for the forgotten card. "I'll take that."

The waitress frowned, looking uncertain. "I don't know. The restaurant policy is—"

"Mr. Hunter and I are close friends, practically family," she assured her, giving the woman what she hoped was a most sincere look. "His niece is my cousin."

"Family, huh?" the waitress asked, her gaze skeptical.

Jasmine nodded. "Family."

"Well, okay." Reluctantly, she handed Jasmine the card. "The bill's still going on his account, with or without his signature."

"I'll be sure to tell him that. Just as soon as I see him again."

Anxious to leave, Jasmine scooted her chair back. Her legs felt wobbly as she stood. The sound of her heart pounded so hard in her ears, she could barely hear the voices of the restaurant patrons around her. Gathering her sweater, she hurried for the exit.

Storm was a man who obviously had pressing things weighing on his mind, proof of which was resting in her hand. She hadn't bought his Casanova routine. Beneath that cool exterior, she sensed there was a man with deep emotions just waiting to be tapped.

It was time she found out if she was right.

Four

Jasmine's heels clicked against the concrete floor, echoing in the quiet night, sounding much too loud in the walkway of the dimly lit hotel. Her stomach fluttered with a mixture of anticipation and trepidation. Thanks to the help of a former classmate working the front desk, she'd learned the room where Storm was staying. Now she just needed the courage to follow through with her decision to find him.

Shakily she inhaled a calming breath. Never before had she had the nerve to follow a man to his hotel room. Especially not a man as overwhelming as Storm Hunter. Defiance, pure and simple, had brought her here. Earlier, before abandoning her at the restaurant, Storm had told her in no uncertain terms that she was a child. And that he was too much man for her to handle. She was determined to prove him wrong.

Only, what if she was the one who was wrong? If sitting next to him in a crowded restaurant had the power to set her pulse racing and her blood warming, goodness only knew what would happen when they were alone. Especially with no one but herself to save her from his obvious charms. A tiny sliver of excitement traveled down her spine, setting second thoughts tumbling around in her confused mind.

Too soon, Room 147 came into sight. Jasmine slowed her pace. She swallowed hard at the lump in her throat as she studied the black numbers on the faded gray door. Gathering her flagging courage, forcing herself to move, she lifted a trembling hand to knock.

Seconds seemed like hours before Storm answered the door. The shocked look on his face was almost worth the butterflies dancing in her stomach. Taking advantage of his stunned state, she eyed him from head to toe. Sans jacket, he still wore the lightweight black sweater and the pleated charcoal gray pants from dinner, both of which emphasized his dark coloring, the width of his shoulders and the slenderness of his hips.

He looked dangerously handsome.

Storm's expression slowly changed. Impatience replaced his surprise. He glared at her, his face darkening with ill-temper. "What are you doing here?"

Jasmine winced inwardly. Not quite the welcome greeting she'd hoped for.

"What I'm doing is a favor for you. Though I doubt if you'll be grateful," she said, her calm voice belying her jittery nerves. The gold credit card glittered in the light streaming out from the door of his room as she held it up for his inspection. "Remember this?"

Recognition flickered in his dark eyes.

A satisfied smile stole across her face. "It would seem this time *I've* got something that belongs to *you.*"

With an irritated breath, he reached for the card.

Jasmine sidestepped his attempt to reclaim his property. Instead she brushed past him into the room, her body sizzling wherever they touched. The musky scent of his cologne filled her nostrils, making her light-headed. Second thoughts pushed their way into her mind, forcing her to reconsider her actions.

What in the world was she thinking? Did she have any idea what she was getting herself into?

Ignoring the nagging voice of reason, she continued her single-minded trek until she stood in the middle of the room, inches from the king-size bed. Only then did she turn to look at him.

His hands on his hips, he stared at her in disbelief. His big body dwarfed the small room, making him appear even more formidable. The scowl on his face did little to settle her qualms of uncertainty. Finally, his voice deep and forbidding, he said, "There must be a misunderstanding. I don't recall inviting you inside."

She forced a smile. "Well, now that I'm here, I think it'd be a perfect time for us to continue our discussion."

"There's nothing more we have to say to each other, Ms. Monroe."

"Wrong again, Mr. Hunter." Her attempt at a lighthearted chuckle sounded strained even to her own ears. "You do have a tendency to jump to the wrong conclusions, don't you?"

His eyes narrowed. "When have I been wrong?"

"Lots of times. This evening, for one. You said you were a man of many…" Her voice caught beneath the strain of his unwavering gaze. Nervously, she licked her lips, then plunged on. "Of many experiences. And that I wasn't old enough to handle someone like you. Well, I beg to differ. I may look young, but I assure you, I'm old enough. I'm not scared of you, Mr. Hunter. No matter how hard you try to frighten me away."

He raised one dark brow. "Are you sure you're not scared?"

She shook her head, not trusting herself to answer.

With exaggerated care, he closed the door. His eyes never leaving her face, he stepped toward her. "I want you to be absolutely certain, Jasmine."

He spoke her name slowly, softly, drawing it out like a caress. She shivered, feeling as though he'd physically touched her.

"Because in another moment," he said as he narrowed the distance between them, "it'll be too late to change your mind."

The hairs on the back of her neck lifted. Goose

bumps speckled her skin, her body's way of warning her what her heart didn't want to accept. Despite all of her blustering to the contrary, she knew she wasn't ready to deal with someone as sensuous and as strong-willed as Storm Hunter.

Before she could give voice to her second thoughts, he was standing in front of her. She felt frozen to the spot, unable to move, watching him. Gently he lifted a hand and stroked her face with the knuckles of his fingers, letting them travel down her cheek, her chin, stopping only to settle at the slender column of her throat.

Shockwaves of desire coursed through her body. She closed her eyes and gasped at the shuddering impact of his soft touch.

The sound shattered the strained silence.

Suddenly the mood shifted, letting the pent-up gates of tension explode wide open. A primal growl of frustration sounded low in Storm's throat. With a ragged breath, he slipped his fingers behind her neck and pulled her roughly toward him.

Her hands were caught between them, pinned against the solid strength of his body. She felt winded, her breath stolen by the quickness of his actions.

Before she could protest, he took her mouth with a savageness that both scared and aroused her. His kiss was hot, possessive. Impatiently he stroked her lips with his tongue, forcing her to open to his demands. She was unable to stop him. He plundered and took with a fierceness that sent heat and awareness throbbing through her.

His big hands slid up and down the length of her body, grazing her breasts, cupping her derriere. Her sweater slid from her shoulders, falling in a silken puddle to the floor. Pulling her snug against him, she felt the hardness of his body, the strength of his arousal. His touch was intimate, turning her muscles to jelly and setting her blood on fire. She clung to him, feeling weak with undeniable desire.

But this wasn't what she'd intended.

She'd thought her first time with Storm, with any man for that matter, would be different. She had wanted it to be special, not a groping match in a hotel room. The embrace felt wrong, sullied in its intent.

"No," she whispered, dragging her mouth from his. Knowing she'd been the catalyst to this onslaught of passion, she turned her head, unable to meet his gaze. Greedily, he took advantage. His lips brushed her neck, nibbling the sensitive spot behind her ear. His breath felt hot against her skin, his tongue warm and moist. Her body trembled at his probing caress.

Shamed by her lack of willpower, she tried to push him away. But she couldn't find the strength to accomplish the task.

He seemed unaware of her change of heart, holding her tighter, his hands growing even bolder. He fumbled with the top snap of her dress.

Desire and fear rose up inside her as she heard the

rasp of her zipper. She felt torn by the clashing emotions, weakened by her own inability to think, or to act. Finally, a whimper of a plea escaped her lips. "Storm, stop…please, stop."

Through the firestorm of passion crackling in his ears, he barely heard the soft whisper of her voice.

"No, Storm. Not now, not like this."

As if drugged by the intoxicating lure of her body, he struggled with his own desires. He forced himself to pull away, to put an unwanted distance between them. His body burned, aching with a need for release. With the loss of her body heat, cool air slapped against his hot skin, chilling him, making him realize just how close he'd come to losing complete control.

Even now, as he stared down at her and saw the evidence of his mindless assault, he knew he still teetered on the edge of repeating his lapse in judgment. Her lips were red and swollen, her hair and makeup mussed, her clothes rumpled. She was trembling. Self-consciously she wrapped her arms around her waist and held herself tightly. She looked so young, so far out of her element.

Jasmine had taken him up on his challenge. Wisely or not, she'd come here to prove herself mature enough to handle him. He'd intended to teach her a lesson. To show her that there was a difference between tempting a man and a boy. Only the lesson had backfired. He'd been the one to be seduced. Holding her in his arms, he'd lost all sense of restraint. If she hadn't stopped him...

Storm clenched his jaw against the anger rising up inside him. Anger directed more at himself than at her. No matter how bold she'd been in coming here, he should have known she wasn't prepared for what had happened. She was just a child, a scared, frightened child. And instead of sending her packing out the door, he'd taken advantage of her naiveté.

"I warned you," he said, unable to keep the accusation from his voice. Remorse made his tone bitter. "I told you you weren't ready."

"Not for this. I didn't know—" Her voice broke as she looked up at him. Moist tears filled her big green eyes. Her chin trembled as she struggled for composure. "I hadn't expected—"

"To be treated like a woman?" The corner of his mouth lifted into a sardonic grin. "What did you expect when you came here to my hotel room, Jasmine? That I'd be a gentleman? That I'd treat you like a prom queen? With kid gloves and genteel manners?"

Her face flushed a deep rosy hue.

"I'm not one of your wet-behind-the-ear suitors." His cynical smile faded. "Or did you forget? I'm an Indian. Honor isn't supposed to be high on my list of qualities, is it?"

Before she could answer, he moved to step around her, heading for the door. As he brushed past, she flinched, shrinking away from him. Storm's heart tightened at the fear he saw in her eyes.

Not allowing himself to reconsider, he threw open the door and turned to face her. "I warned you I wasn't to be trusted," he said, the words harsh even to his own ears. "Now run, Jasmine. Run before I change my mind and take what you were so willing to offer."

Blinking back tears of shame and embarrassment, she refused to look at him. Instead, with her eyes downcast, she stumbled to the door and escaped into the night.

For a long moment he stood in the doorway and listened to the rapid click of her heels as she ran down the walkway from his room. He listened until the distant taps faded to a dull and painful memory. Then he closed the door and leaned against its solid strength.

Shutting his eyes, he sighed wearily. He'd made such a mess of things. From the very beginning, Jasmine had been nothing but honest about her feelings toward him. Instead of returning the favor, he'd used those feelings against her. He'd been too afraid to face his own emotions. Too afraid to admit that he might be attracted to her.

Like a bully, he'd used his size and brute strength to frighten her. As a result, he'd destroyed the self-confidence of a woman who'd shown him nothing but respect. Ironically, Jasmine was the only person in town who hadn't treated him like a specter from the past.

His heart thumped a hollow beat against his chest. Opening his eyes, he glanced around the room, forcing himself to face the scene of his own crime. He frowned as he spotted something white on the floor in the middle of the mauve carpeting. He pushed himself away from the door.

It was Jasmine's sweater.

Reluctantly, he picked it up and held it in his hands. The delicate material felt silky, cool to his touch, reminding him of Jasmine's smooth skin. Burying his face in the sweater's softness, he inhaled its sweet floral scent and felt as though he were still holding her close in his arms.

A sharp and jagged pain jigsawed through his heart as he realized what a fool he had been. Even now he couldn't admit the truth, just how much he had wanted her to stay.

He hadn't wanted to let her go.

Gravel spewed from the tires of Jasmine's Jeep as she made the turn too quickly into the long driveway of the Big Sky Bed & Breakfast. Easing up on the gas pedal, she told herself to slow down. That no matter how much she wanted to she couldn't run away from what had just happened.

Her headlights cut a narrow beam through the thick darkness. She shivered as cool, crisp air poured in

through the open window. A complete and utter stillness filled the night, doing little to quiet the troubling
thoughts echoing in her head.

There was no denying she'd made a fool of herself
over a man. Not just any man, but Storm Hunter. A
man who held her entire family in such disdain.

She gave a bittersweet smile. Well, she'd certainly
done little to change his opinion of her. Or the Kincaid clan, for that matter. If anything, she'd given him
even more reason to believe the worst of them. He'd
made her feel like a spoiled child who couldn't handle
not getting her own way.

Once again Jasmine felt the tears well up in her
eyes. She pounded a fist against the steering wheel,
refusing to give them release. Her feminine pride
wouldn't allow the show of weakness.

Silently she vowed no man would ever make her
cry.

A light shone from the front porch of the B and B.
Upstairs, the guest rooms were dark, their occupants
asleep for the night. Navigating her Jeep around to
the side of the house, she parked and let herself in
the back door.

Thankfully, the kitchen was empty. At the moment
she didn't think she could face her mother. She was
in no mood for another lecture. Slipping off her heels,
she tiptoed through the dark and silent house. Midway
up the stairs to the third floor, a loose board creaked

beneath her weight. She froze, straining her ears for signs of life.

The house remained quiet.

Relieved, she continued upstairs, longing for a soak in a hot tub. After her encounter with Storm, she felt dirty, soiled. Disappointment rested heavily against her heart, making it hard to draw a breath. Disappointment not because of what had happened, but because of what hadn't.

Despite everything, she couldn't shake the feeling that she and Storm had missed a chance at something special. Perhaps it was just wishful thinking on her part, but she still believed they were meant to be together.

Wearily, she moved past her sister Cleo's empty bedroom. The light shining from beneath her mother's door told her she wasn't asleep. Guiltily, instead of stopping to say good-night, she continued on. Jasmine took only two steps past before her mother's door swung open, startling her. In the swath of light coming from the room, her mother stood in the doorway, wrapped in a cream-colored dressing gown.

"Jasmine, it's late." Concern laced her mother's voice. "Where have you been?"

Instinctively, Jasmine backed away from the light, unwilling to let her mother see her disheveled appearance. "Dinner, Mother. I told you I was going to meet Summer—"

"Summer called nearly an hour ago. She wanted

to make sure you'd gotten home all right. And to apologize for having to cut dinner short.''

Jasmine nearly moaned in dismay. Earlier this evening she'd told her mother she'd be dining with Summer and Gavin. Not wanting to upset her mother further, she hadn't mentioned her other dinner companion, Storm. Now, barring another lie of omission, she had no excuse for her tardiness.

''Is anything wrong, Jasmine? Why are you hovering in the dark? Come closer, where I can see you.''

Reluctantly, Jasmine stepped forward.

Her mother's sharp gaze scanned her from head to toe, lingering on her mussed hair, her swollen lips and rumpled dress. With a tsk, she shook her head. ''You've been with that man, haven't you?''

'' 'That man'?'' Used to her open-mindedness and free thinking, Jasmine was stunned by the condemnation in her mother's tone. ''He has a name, Mother. It's Storm Hunter.''

''I know his name. I know all about him and his family,'' she said, her voice quavering, her expression hard. ''I told you to stay away from him. He's too old for you, Jasmine.''

''Too old? Mother, I can't believe you'd mean that.''

''I refuse to argue with you.'' Celeste turned from the doorway. In a flurry of cotton and lace, she swept across the carpeted length of her bedroom floor.

Reluctantly, Jasmine followed her inside.

Candles lined the fireplace, setting shadows dancing against the floral-and-striped wallpaper. The pungent scent of incense spiced the air, telling her that her mother had once again been calling upon the spiritual world for guidance.

"Why can't you understand?" Celeste demanded, calling her attention. "It would never work between the two of you. You and Storm come from two entirely different worlds."

"Surely you don't mean because he's a Native American?"

"No, of course not," Celeste said impatiently. She stopped, narrowing a gaze to study her. "I'm talking about life experiences. You're so young, Jasmine. He's nearly twice your age. Is it any wonder that I'd be concerned?"

"Mother, really." Jasmine sighed. First Storm. Now her mother. When would everyone stop bringing up her age as though it were a handicap? "I'm not a child. Nor am I completely inexperienced. You know as well as I do that I've been dating since I was sixteen."

"You've dated men your own age. That isn't the same as seeing a man as old as Storm Hunter."

"No, it isn't. It's better." Ignoring her mother's shocked expression, she added, "Mother, I've never felt the way I do when I'm with Storm. Not with any other man. You're right. He is different. But not in a bad way."

Her mother's hand shook as she raised it to her throat. She looked stricken. "I don't want to hear this. How can you even consider a relationship with him? There's too dark a history between the Hunters and the Kincaids. It wasn't all that long ago that his brother's affair with my sister nearly destroyed my family. I lost my sister because of Raven Hunter. I won't stand by and let it happen again."

"Mother, that was another time, and another place. Prejudices of the past stood in Raven and Blanche's way, not their love for each other. Blanche died from complications of childbirth. There wasn't anything anyone could have done. It wasn't Storm's fault. Nor was it Raven's—"

"Stop!" Celeste's eyes took on a wide-eyed fear-fulness that Jasmine had never seen before. "I don't want to talk about Raven. I just want you to promise me that you'll never see Storm again."

Jasmine stared at her, too stunned to speak. Finally, after a long moment, she shook her head and said, "It's too late, Mother. You don't need to worry. None of this really matters, anyway."

Celeste frowned. "What are you talking about?"

"I'm talking about Storm…and me." The ever-present tears filled her eyes. With a humorless laugh, she raked a hand through her short, cropped hair. "You're too late with your advice, Mother. Storm has made it perfectly clear that he isn't interested in me.

In fact after tonight I doubt if he'll ever want to see me again.''

Her mother took a step toward her. ''Jasmine, I'm sorry—''

''No, Mother.'' Jasmine held up a hand, stopping her. ''I don't want to hear any words of sympathy. I wouldn't believe them, anyway.''

Celeste blinked, looking wounded by the accusation. ''Jasmine, you're not being fair.''

''No, I suppose I'm not,'' Jasmine said, choking back a sob. ''Pardon me, but I'm not feeling very gracious at the moment.''

''I love you, darling,'' Celeste said, wringing her fingers. ''You know I care—''

''Sometimes you care too much. You worry too much about me, Mother. It's time you let me make my own decisions…and my own mistakes. It's time you let me go.''

With that, she turned from her mother's room. Refusing to look back, she escaped down the night-darkened hall. She felt weary beyond words, her feet leadened as she strode to her bedroom. Her heart throbbed painfully in her chest.

Tears blurred her vision as she fumbled with the knob. Thankfully the door finally opened and she hurried inside. Closing it behind her, she bolted the lock, in no mood to risk any more company.

With only the moonlight to guide her, she stumbled to the window seat that overlooked Blue Mirror Lake.

A silvery glow lit the surface of the lake, shimmering like diamonds in the soft, cloudless night. In the distance she saw the outline of the mountains of Laughing Horse Reservation.

Once again, she was reminded of Storm Hunter.

She felt his presence as though he were in the room with her at that very moment. It would take a long time, perhaps forever, before she could forget the chiseled angles of his handsome face, the dark and penetrating beauty of his eyes, or the determined set of his strong chin.

A tear slid down her cheek, followed closely by another, then another. Unable to help herself, Jasmine did what she swore she would never allow. Hugging a chintz pillow to her chest, she gave in to a much-needed bout of tears.

In the safety of the empty room, she mourned the loss of a man she'd never even had the right to call her own.

Five

At nine o'clock the next morning Storm paced the floor of his hotel room. The floral-papered walls were beginning to close in around him. He felt as restless as a caged animal. He'd been up and prowling for so long his footsteps were permanently imprinted on the mauve carpeting.

"Dammit, what am I supposed to do now?" he growled, his deep voice echoing hollowly in the empty room. Frustrated, he plowed long fingers through his hair, raking the dark strands from his face. Instead of focusing on what he'd come to Whitehorn to accomplish, uncovering the truth behind his brother's murder, he'd been distracted by thoughts of a woman. Since sending Jasmine fleeing into the night, he'd been unable to relax, to sleep, to do anything but think about what a complete and utter fool he'd been. In his attempt to discourage her interest in him, he'd frightened and shamed her. While his intentions may have been honest, his delivery had been cruel.

Now guilt rested uneasily upon his shoulders.

Storm reluctantly forced his gaze to the phone. He

had no choice, he realized. He had to speak to her again. He had to apologize for his behavior. If he didn't, he would forever be haunted by the hurt, disillusioned look in her eyes.

Sighing, he glanced at the bedside clock and decided now was as good a time as any to call. Jasmine lived and worked at the B and B. Surely she'd be up and about, seeing to the needs of her guests.

His stomach tightened as he crossed the room to the nightstand. He sat down heavily on the edge of the unmade bed, with its mauve and blue print bedcovers. Picking up the phone, he sucked in a breath of courage, then punched in the number for the Big Sky Bed & Breakfast.

Listening to the phone ring, once, twice, three times, it suddenly occurred to him that Jasmine might not be the one to pick up the receiver. After all, she wasn't the only member of her family working at the bed-and-breakfast. Storm tensed, unnerved by the thought. What was he supposed to say if her mother answered? Remembering Celeste's skittish reaction to his appearance at the sheriff's office, fainting dead in David Hannon's arms, he doubted she would be overjoyed by his early morning call.

Before he could reconsider, the phone was picked up. "Big Sky Bed & Breakfast," a familiar voice chimed.

Relief eased the tension from his muscles. "Jasmine?"

Deafening silence was his only response.

Undaunted, he said, ''Jasmine, it's Storm Hunter.''

''I know.''

The two simple words spoke volumes as to her frame of mind. Obviously she had not forgotten, nor forgiven, what had happened between them last night.

Refusing to be discouraged, he tried again. ''I'd like to talk to you.''

''I'm listening.''

He hesitated. Considering the coolness of her tone, he knew in his heart this was one apology he must make in person. ''If you don't mind, I'd rather meet with you.''

Once again silence stretched across the phone line. For a heart-stopping moment, Storm thought she'd hung up on him. ''Jasmine?'' he said, unable to hide the fear from his tone. ''Are you still there?''

''Yes, I'm still here.'' Her soft whisper of a sigh set his senses prickling with awareness. ''I'm just not sure if it would be wise for us to have any more contact, Mr. Hunter.''

Mr. Hunter. He winced at the formal use of his name. Last night, she'd called him Storm. It would seem they'd taken one step forward, two steps back. She wasn't going to make this easy for him. Not that he deserved otherwise.

''I don't see that we have much of a choice. I have your sweater. You left it here last night,'' he countered, using any excuse within his means to see her again. He hoped he didn't sound as anxious as he felt. "I feel I should return it to you. If you want, I could stop by the B and B—"

"No, I'll meet you," she said quickly. Too quickly, leaving little doubt of his welcome at her home.

But her family's feelings toward him didn't matter, he told himself, almost smiling his relief. What mattered was that Jasmine had finally relented; she had agreed to see him. "Just tell me when and where."

"In an hour. There's a lookout in the mountains overlooking Crazy Peak. It's a popular spot with the locals. But I doubt if anyone will be there this morning."

No, they wouldn't. The lookout would be busy after nightfall. If memory served, it was popular with young lovers—Native American and Anglo alike—looking for a place to be alone, he mused silently. Frowning, he wondered which of her young suitors had taken her to this notorious makeout point.

Out loud, he said, "I know the place. I'll be there in an hour."

Without another word, Jasmine hung up the phone.

For a long moment Storm didn't move. He listened to the tinny silence humming in his ear, until the warning beep of a disconnected phone line sounded. Only then did he return the receiver to its cradle.

Obviously, Jasmine was still upset. Rightly so.

It would take more than a simple apology to convince her of his remorse. A task that shouldn't be hard, considering his life's work as a lawyer hinged on his power of persuasion. Storm's frown deepened. So, why did it feel as though he'd just taken on the toughest case of his life?

Why did he feel as though his last chance of finding peace and contentment rested on the outcome of his meeting with Jasmine?

One hour later, her heart heavy with regret, Jasmine drove her Jeep into the foothills of the Crazy Mountains. With the top down on the Wrangler, a brisk wind buffeted her skin, bringing tears to her eyes. At least that was the only excuse she allowed herself for the show of emotion. For the first time in her life, she had lied to her mother. Instead of being honest and telling her she was going to meet Storm, she had used an errand as an excuse to leave the B and B.

Lying and deceiving didn't come easily to her. By her mother's example, she'd been taught to live her life honestly, openly. At times, perhaps, too openly. There were those in Whitehorn who believed her family to be eccentric. The reminder brought on a familiar burr of irritation, which Jasmine forced aside. She didn't care what others thought. She'd rather be considered odd than live her life in the rigid confines of closed-minded conformity.

The road narrowed, demanding her attention. With the ease of experience, she negotiated the steep curves. The air felt cool, thick with the scent of the pine trees that lined the road. Ever since she'd been a child, the Crazies had been her favorite place to visit. Even now, when things got too hectic in real life, she escaped to the mountains, finding peace and solace in their rugged peaks. Her mother's explanation for her beguilement was that she'd lived a past life in the mountains, perhaps as a goatherder or a trapper.

The thought brought a reluctant smile as she considered her mother's off-centered influence upon her life. The first year of their marriage, her parents lived in Baton Rouge. Then Celeste had convinced Ty to return to Whitehorn to raise Summer. From then on, even after Ty's death, Celeste uniquely shaped all of their lives—hers, Cleo's and Summer's—by stressing the importance of free-spirited independence.

When they were old enough to toddle off on their own, Celeste had pushed them out the door to experience all the world had to offer. She'd encouraged them to think for themselves and to voice their own opinions. A philosophy that, to the chagrin of others in the community, Jasmine had embraced wholeheartedly.

In first grade, wanting to be like the cowboys she'd seen on her uncle Jeremiah's ranch, Jasmine had refused to give up her boots for a more appropriate pair of Mary Jane shoes. Only Celeste's promise to host a class field trip on the grounds of the Blue Mirror

Lake had convinced the principle to bend the rules of the dress code.

During her sophomore year in high school, the dissection of a frog had been a requirement for biology class. Appalled at the idea of such inhumane treatment of a helpless creature, Jasmine had refused to do anything so cruel. Not only had her mother applauded her decision, but Celeste and her aunt Yvette had joined her protest by holding a sit-in on the school steps. Despite their help, she'd failed the lab section of the class, ending up with C for the course. But together they had scored a victory in the name of family solidarity.

When Jasmine had blossomed into womanhood, her mother had gone beyond the usual birds-and-the-bees speech. When other mothers were blushing at the mention of sex, Celeste had left no doubt in her young daughter's mind what a healthy relationship between a man and woman ought to be. Not only that, but she'd made sure Jasmine was aware of the methods of birth control available to her should she decide the time was right.

Instead of encouraging her to be promiscuous, her mother's openness had left Jasmine with an overwhelming sense of responsibility. She'd taken to heart the trust she'd been given, by deciding to remain a virgin until she met the man she intended to marry.

Now, at the age of twenty-three, she was still waiting for the right man.

Unbidden, Storm Hunter's handsome image cropped up in her mind's eye. The thought of seeing him again left her confused and uncertain. In Storm she thought she'd found that perfect man, that she was ready to take that giant step of trust. But last night in his hotel room Storm had proven to her that she wasn't nearly as worldly as she'd like for him to believe. Nor as brave as she would have liked to have believed for herself.

He'd hurt her deeply.

Not physically so much as emotionally.

Rejection was painful, but most especially at the hands of someone such as Storm, a man with whom she'd felt such an instant and strong connection. Fresh tears pressed against her eyes. Jasmine blinked hard, fighting their release. She wasn't sure of the reason behind Storm's unexpected request to see her again. But one thing was for certain, her pride would never allow him to see just how much he had wounded her.

Cornering the next curve too sharply, Jasmine's tires squealed in protest. Shifting to a lower gear, she slowed the Jeep to a more manageable speed, concentrating on the road ahead. Too soon, she arrived at her destination. Her heart thumped painfully against her breast as she pulled into the lookout's parking lot.

Storm was waiting for her.

He stood outside his car, leaning against its silver finish. This morning he'd dressed in a pair of casual but expensively labeled jeans and a polo shirt. He wore loafers with no socks and looked as though he'd stepped off the cover of a *GQ* magazine. He was the perfect advertisement for the professional man at ease.

Kicking up a cloud of dust in her wake, Jasmine parked her Jeep next to his car. Letting the dust settle, she slowly unhooked her seat belt. Turning his head, he watched as she stepped down onto the graveled lot. A light wind ruffled his long hair. Mirrored sunglasses hid his expressive dark eyes from view. His chiseled face remained somber, revealing none of his emotions.

Daunted, she stopped short of joining him, leaving a small but safe distance between them. But even with that, he was so blatantly male, she couldn't help but feel a primal pull of attraction.

For a long moment they stood staring at each other, neither seeming to know what to say. With each passing second, awareness grew inside her, until she thought she might explode with the unwanted tension.

Storm was the first to break the spell of silence. His deep voice startled her when he finally said, ''Thank you for coming.''

He sounded so frank, so earnest. She almost believed he meant it…almost. His harsh rejection still echoed in her mind. Forgetting her resolve to remain aloof, she blurted, ''Why did you call? After last night I thought I'd be the last person you'd want to see.''

"Last night was a mistake," he said, slipping the sunglasses from the bridge of his nose. He tossed them through the car's open window onto the dashboard, then pushed himself away from the door. Taking a step toward her, he held her in his gaze. "I'm not in the habit of ravishing young women. Things got out of hand. My behavior was uncalled for. I hope you'll accept my apology. I assure you it won't happen again."

Jasmine felt a confusing mix of relief and disappointment. Standing here, close enough that she could almost touch him, she couldn't deny that she was still deeply attracted to him. Yet, looking into his expressive eyes, she saw nothing but sincerity in their depths. She believed him when he said things had gotten out of hand. Unfortunately, she also believed him when he said it wouldn't happen again.

Still, a part of her wasn't ready to settle for just an apology. Last night he'd acted as though he'd wanted to punish her, to punish himself for wanting her. Once and for all she needed to know why.

"Why are you so determined to dislike me?"

Emotion flickered in his eyes. Averting his gaze, he stared out at the scenic mountain view, watching as clouds scudded past the white-tipped peaks. He remained silent for so long, she thought he'd decided not to answer. Until he inhaled a deep breath, then released it with a whistling sigh. "It's not that I dislike you. It's that—" He stopped, his jaw clenching reflexively. A tiny vein pulsed at his temple. Still unable to face her, he continued, "Too much has happened between our families. Our pasts are connected in a way that makes it impossible for us to do anything but remain on opposite sides. I'm sure you must realize this."

Jasmine's breath caught painfully in her throat. She wanted to argue, but couldn't find the words. Perhaps he was right. Theirs was a dark history, one that couldn't easily be forgotten. Making amends now, after all that had happened, seemed too little, too late.

Unwilling to give up, she said, "We weren't the ones to start the feud between our families. Why should we keep it alive after all this time?"

He looked at her, his gaze so direct, so penetrating, she felt as though he could see inside to her very soul. "My brother died because he fell in love with the wrong woman, a white woman. I'm not going to make the same mistake."

Jasmine met his gaze, unable to look away. She considered his answer, deciding if they'd come this far, she couldn't turn back now. Steeling herself for his condemnation, she stated the obvious. "You blame me and my family for your brother's death."

She saw the flash of pain in his eyes. Lying badly, he said, "I don't know who's responsible for Raven's death. Because of the circumstances surrounding his murder, we may never know the truth. And for that reason, I'm afraid my brother's soul will never find peace.''

"Circumstances? You mean justice won't be served because there may be a Kincaid involved?''

Storm's lips formed a thin, tight line. He refused to answer.

But he didn't have to. They both knew the truth. The Kincaid name was a powerful influence in this area. Powerful enough to put a murder investigation into permanent limbo, if the motivation was great enough. No matter how much wealth he may have acquired since leaving town, or how many connections he might have made as a lawyer in New Mexico, they both knew Storm's reputation meant nothing here in Whitehorn.

"I can't tell you who is or who's not involved," he said, his tone sounding defeated. "I can't get close enough to the investigation to find out the truth.''

Jasmine felt his frustration as though it were her own. Her heart swelled with compassion for the pain she saw in his eyes. She blamed herself and her family for putting him through this turmoil. There was only one solution. One way to end his suffering, once and for all.

Surprising them both, she made her offer, "I'm going to help you, Storm. We're going to uncover the identity of your brother's murderer together.''

"Do you have any idea what you're proposing?'' Storm asked, his voice sharper than he'd intended.

"I'm proposing an alliance," she said. The calmness with which she spoke clashed against turbulent emotions churning inside him. "I think if we tried, we could work together as a team."

"A team?" He stared at her, unable to believe his ears.

Despite the obvious reason why an alliance between them would not work—namely, the unwanted attraction that sprung up whenever they were near—there was an even more compelling reason to refuse. She was a Kincaid, offering to help him find out the truth behind his brother's murder. There was obviously a conflict of interest.

He didn't know whether to trust her or to suspect her motives, as he'd learned to suspect all white men's motives.

But then again, this was Jasmine. A woman who, as he was quickly finding out, was nothing if not painfully honest. From their few encounters, she didn't appear able to lie, even if she'd wanted to.

"The whole idea is ridiculous," he said in a dismissive tone. Gravel crunched beneath his shoes as he turned on his heel and spun away from her, eager to leave and put a much-needed distance between himself and temptation.

"Please hear me out, Storm," she said, reaching a hand to stop him.

Her palm felt warm, soft, as she wrapped her fingers around his wrist. Arrows of heat and awareness darted up his forearm. He flinched at the unexpected contact. Slowly his gaze traveled from her hand up to her face. There, in the depths of her green eyes, he saw an innocence that nearly took his breath away.

It wasn't an act. Her proposition, as impossible as it might be, was for real. She really wanted to help him.

"What's wrong with my wanting to help you?" she asked, echoing his own thoughts.

He tightened his jaw against his weakening resolve. "I don't need your help, Jasmine. I don't need anyone's help. Whatever I've achieved in my life, I've done it on my own terms. The last thing I want is someone else poking their nose into my business out of a sense of pity."

"That's what you think I'm feeling? Pity? How dare you presume to know my own thoughts!" Anger flashed in her eyes. She released his hand, growling her frustration. "At this moment I don't know who to be more angry with—the legal system for refusing to treat you fairly, or you for being so stubborn."

He felt winded, stung by her unfair reprimand. He was the wounded party, not her. Yet, standing awkwardly by the car, he wondered how she'd accomplished the feat. Somehow, once again, she'd made him feel guilty, as though he were the one in the wrong.

"I don't want to argue with you, Jasmine. Arguing is pointless. We both know who killed my brother."

"You mean, Jeremiah Kincaid...my uncle."

"Your *deceased* uncle," he corrected, surprised by her admission. "Jeremiah has been long buried, and his secrets along with him."

"Maybe, maybe not," she countered. "There's only one way to find out for sure. Listen to me, Storm. My cousin, David, is the FBI agent helping with the investigation. We've always been close. If there's any information that the police aren't telling, I'm sure I could find a way for him to confide in me."

Reluctantly, Storm acknowledged what she had to say was the truth. His previous encounters with David Hannon had been strained at best. Frustrated by the investigation's lack of progress, he'd allowed his temper to get the better of him. He'd argued with the man, almost coming to blows over the disagreement.

Oblivious to his wavering thoughts, Jasmine continued, her voice gentle, her tone a plea for reason. "Your brother was last seen alive at the Kincaid ranch. A ranch that now belongs to my cousin, Garrett Kincaid. Alone, you can't get anywhere near that ranch. But as a member of the Kincaids, who would think it odd if I wished to visit the family homestead and bring along a guest?"

Storm released a growl of impatience. "Jasmine—"

"No, wait, there's more. I have an intimate connection to the only surviving person known to be in the house on the night of your brother's murder—my mother." She hesitated, a flush of color stealing across her face. Then, with an honesty to which he'd grown accustomed, she said, "My mother doesn't want me anywhere near you. Just how far do you think you'll get if you try to question her on your own?"

Nowhere fast, he admitted to himself. Since his return to Whitehorn, he'd been stonewalled by the police department. No one seemed to care about him, or his brother's death. Why should they? He was just another annoying Indian. Storm fought the rising tide of bitterness. Jasmine was right. The investigation into Raven's murder was at a virtual standstill.

For years he had lived without knowing what had happened to Raven. His life had been put in limbo. Not knowing whether to be angry and hurt by his brother's abandonment, or to grieve over Raven's death.

Now that he knew what had happened to his brother, he couldn't allow the questions to go unanswered. He could not rest until he uncovered the truth. He had to know why Raven had died, and who was responsible.

"What about last night?" he asked abruptly. "What happened in my hotel room...do you think you could trust me enough to work with me?"

She shrugged, giving an unconvincing attempt at nonchalance. "Like you said, last night was a mistake. We both allowed our emotions to overrule our judgment. It won't happen again.''

He raised a brow. ''You're sure about that?''

''Positive, because I won't allow it.'' She raised her chin in a show of feminine pride. ''Trust me, Storm. I'm not a glutton for punishment. I'm simply not interested in a man who isn't interested in me.''

Not interested was hardly the way he felt. He studied her for a long moment, debating the wisdom of telling her just how wrong her assumption really was. Deciding that some things were best kept to himself, he gave a resigned sigh and said, ''If I were to agree—''

A smile blossomed on her beautiful face. Storm's heart pounded a warning beat in his chest.

''I said *if* I were to agree,'' he repeated firmly. ''You would have to promise me that you wouldn't risk putting yourself into any danger.''

''Danger?'' The sculpted line of her brow furrowed. ''What danger could there be after all these years? Those who were involved are long gone. They can't hurt us now.''

It had been his experience that people would go to great lengths to cover up a family scandal, especially those that had been long buried. ''I just want you to be careful.''

She gave a dismissive shake of the head. ''I will.''

Storm frowned, agitated by her apparent lack of concern. ''When do you want to start?''

Her face brightened. "How about tomorrow?"

He nodded. "Tomorrow, it is."

"I feel like we should celebrate. We've finally agreed on something." Jasmine laughed, her eyes sparkling with mischief. She glanced at her wristwatch and sighed. Her tone shifted from playful to business-like. "Unfortunately I don't have the time. I took an early lunch to meet with you. My mother's waiting for me. I've got to get back to the B and B. I have to make breakfast tomorrow morning for our guests. After that, I should be able to get the rest of the day off. There's no use in both of us driving tomorrow. Why don't I pick you up at your hotel, say around eleven o'clock?"

Second thoughts worked their way into his mind, setting his nerves on edge. Instead of giving in to his doubts, he nodded. "I'll be ready."

With a smile that set fire racing through his veins, she bid him goodbye and strode to her Jeep. Today her long legs were hidden beneath a pair of blue jeans. But that didn't spoil the view. The faded denim clung to her legs and backside like a second skin. His body ached with awareness as he studied the gentle sway of her hips.

Swinging herself up into the driver's seat, she fastened her seatbelt and gunned the motor to life. With one last wave goodbye, she threw the gear into reverse and backed out of the parking space. Spewing dust and rocks, she shifted forward and peeled out, leaving him to stand alone in the middle of the empty lot. He felt her absence like a hollow place in his heart.

At that moment Storm knew, with this new alliance of theirs, he was courting trouble.

He had never met a more beautiful woman. The longer he was with her, the greater his desire for her grew. But even more disturbing than desire, what he felt for her was respect.

As everyone else in town, including the members of her own family, Jasmine could have gone out of her way to avoid him. After all, Raven's death was his problem, not hers. She was under no obligation to help him.

But instead of running away, she'd taken on the responsibility of seeking the truth. She was risking the wrath of her own family to help him. He had never known a woman quite like her.

Desire and respect, Storm mused. In his opinion, the two were a dangerous combination.

Six

Jasmine tugged at the bedcovers, feeling restless and out of sorts. It was late, after two o'clock in the morning, and she hadn't yet been able to relax enough to sleep. Knowing that she'd be up in less than four hours to start breakfast for the B and B's guests made the late hour seem even more daunting.

Each wrinkle in the bed, imagined or otherwise, irritated her. Despite the open windows, there was no cooling breeze filtering inside. The room felt hot and stuffy. Her skin was damp with perspiration. Her head ached with fatigue. She wanted to blame her insomnia on the unusually warm night. But the truth was a guilty conscience had kept her awake.

Sighing, Jasmine sat up in bed. She snapped on the lamp at her bedside table. A soft light washed over her, bringing into focus the room that had been hers since childhood. The dusky green-and-cream striped paper she'd picked out when she was ten years old still hung on the walls. Her grandmother's handmade patchwork quilt covered the dark mission-style bed. Chintz curtains framed the large windows. Matching pillows and a collection of stuffed animals were arranged on the window seat beneath.

The room was as familiar as the back of her hand, as soothing as a hug from an old friend. Yet tonight she could find no comfort in its embrace. Tonight, she felt as though she were a stranger in its midst, as though she didn't belong. Since agreeing to help Storm with his search for the truth behind his brother's death, she felt oddly detached from her home as well as from her own family.

Her eyes burned from lack of sleep. Rubbing them, she leaned back against the pillows and considered the consequences of her decision. In her heart, she knew helping Storm was the right thing to do. No one should have to endure the pain he was suffering. For almost thirty years he'd lived without knowing what had happened to his brother. If she'd lost Cleo or Summer in that way, she'd didn't know if she could survive.

Storm had survived the ordeal.

But not without a price.

This morning she'd heard the bitterness in his voice when he'd told her that he didn't need her help, that he didn't need anyone's help. She had seen the suspicious look in his eyes when she'd pledged her support. Through the years of struggle Storm had learned not to trust anyone. She had to prove her sincerity. No matter how hard he tried to push her way, she couldn't abandon him.

She had to help him.

Even if it meant doing so behind her family's back.

Giving up on sleep, Jasmine pushed aside the sheets and climbed out of bed. Crossing the room to the window seat, she picked up a favorite stuffed animal from her past, Mr. Truckles, a well-loved bunny with lopsided ears, patchy fur and a nose that was almost completely worn off. She hugged the stuffed rabbit to her chest and sat on the cushioned seat. Tucking her long legs beneath her, she peered outside into the dark night.

Clouds blocked the moon's shimmering light, casting the lake into a murky darkness. The night seemed too black, too forbidding, putting her nerves even further on edge. She didn't know how she was going to get through the next few days, helping Storm without telling her mother the truth. Now that Cleo and Summer were married, her mother had come to rely upon her even more. Jasmine felt a keen sense of responsibility for her mother's well-being. It wasn't any wonder that telling lies didn't sit well with her conscience.

An ear-piercing scream shattered the silence, jolting her out of her troubled thoughts.

In her haste to stand, Jasmine nearly tumbled from her seat at the window. Catching herself, she scrambled to her feet and stood frozen in the middle of the room, with her heart pounding and her ears straining to listen to the sudden quiet that surrounded her. For a moment she thought she must have heard the screech of an owl, or had even imagined the cry.

Then it sounded again.

This time she knew it was from inside the house. The scream had come from her mother's bedroom.

She dropped Mr. Truckles back onto the window seat and in two quick steps was at the door. Fumbling with the knob, she tore it open and ran blindly down the night-darkened hall. Her mother's bedroom door was closed, but, thankfully, not locked. The bedside lamp was still on, guiding her. An opened book, with her mother's reading glasses beside it, had been placed on the bedside table. A white candle was lit, softly shimmering in the dim light beside her. Her mother was propped up in bed against a cushion of pillows, looking as though she'd fallen asleep while reading.

But her expression was anything but restful.

Agony twisted the beautiful, care-worn features of her face. Her complexion was ashen, her russet hair tousled. With her eyes still tightly closed, she thrashed her head from side to side, as though trying to rid herself of a nightmare.

Celeste was dreaming, Jasmine realized.

Her step faltering, she hesitated, not sure whether to wake her mother. Afraid that she'd scare her more if she did. But another cry of alarm settled her indecision. Jasmine hurried to her mother's side. She placed a hand on Celeste's shoulder and shook her gently.

Celeste woke with a start. Her eyes wild and frightened, she stared at Jasmine, as though she were looking through her, not at her. Her body trembled with fear. Her chest rose sharply, as she sucked in a shuddering breath.

"Mother, are you all right?" Jasmine asked, unable to keep the tremor of fear from her own voice.

Celeste opened and closed her mouth, but no sound was emitted. Looking as though she were seeing a ghost, she stared at her daughter. Finally, her voice sounding as hoarse and dry as the wind on the plains, she whispered, "Blanche?"

Jasmine's heart stuttered. "No, Mother. It's me—"

"Blanche, it's been so long." Celeste reached out a shaky hand and touched Jasmine's cheek. Tears welled up in her eyes. Her breath catching on a sob, she said, "Oh, Blanche...don't be angry. I'm so sorry, so very sorry. I never meant for it to happen. Please...please forgive me."

"Forgive you?" Jasmine frowned, her concern growing. "For what, Mother?"

Celeste closed her eyes and shook her head. "No, I—I can't talk about it. I won't. Do you hear me? I won't."

Jasmine's heart slammed against her chest. A lump of dread lodged in her throat. Desperate, she gathered her mother's hands in hers and said, "Mother, look at me. Open your eyes and look at me."

Celeste's eyes slowly opened, though the wild, frightened look still remained.

"Can you see me, Mother? It's Jasmine, not Blanche. Jasmine, your daughter."

Celeste's expression shifted. The terror burning in her eyes dimmed. She blinked, quick rapid blinks, as though trying to bring the room into focus. "Jasmine?"

Relief surged through her body. "Yes, it's Jasmine."

"W-what happened? What's wrong?" Celeste struggled to sit up.

Jasmine placed a hand on her mother's shoulder, quieting her. "Just lie back and relax for a moment. You were having a nightmare."

"A nightmare," Celeste repeated, frowning in confusion. "I don't remember. I—I couldn't sleep, so I decided to read." Her frown deepened, the pitch of her voice rising anxiously. She pushed the hair from her eyes and searched Jasmine's face. "I must have dozed off, but I just don't remember."

"It's okay, Mother. Everything's all right now. You just scared me for a moment."

Tears slid down Celeste's cheeks. "I'm so sorry, darling. I didn't mean to disturb you."

"Don't be silly. There's no need to be sorry.

You've been under such a strain lately. I just wish I could help you."

Celeste didn't answer. Instead, lifting a hand, she wiped the telltale moisture from her face and struggled to compose herself.

"Do you want to talk about your dream?" Jasmine persisted, unwilling to let her mother avoid what had happened. "It might help."

Celeste shook her head. "No, I—I can't."

"Mother, you called me Blanche."

"Blanche?" Her red-rimmed eyes widened in alarm.

Choosing her words carefully, Jasmine explained, "When I woke you, you looked at me so strangely, like you weren't really seeing me. Then you called me Blanche."

Celeste sat up abruptly. She brushed the covers aside and swung her shapely legs off the bed. Rising stiffly to her feet, she waved off Jasmine's offer to help. "I'll be all right, Jasmine. I just need to get up and stretch my legs."

"Mother, you're not all right," Jasmine said, giving an exasperated breath. "You just had a terrible nightmare. Why won't you talk to me about it?"

"It won't do any good to talk about it now. It's over...done with. I just want to forget about it." Celeste crossed the room to the fireplace. There, with a trembling hand, she lit a match and began to light the numerous candles scattered about on the nightstand and mantel.

Jasmine sighed. First the candles, then the oil would be next. Then, as was too often the case, instead of confiding in her daughter, Celeste would turn to the spiritual world for comfort. Though Jasmine knew she was wasting her time, she asked once again, "Mother, are you sure there's nothing I can do to help you?"

From a vial on her nightstand, Celeste poured out a dollop of bergamot oil and rubbed it into her left hand. "Jasmine, there's no need to worry," she said, her voice regaining some of its former confidence, though the dark circles under her eyes and the drawn features of her face did little to allay Jasmine's concerns. "I just need some time alone. I hope you understand."

"Yes, of course," Jasmine said numbly. She understood all too well. As she had done so often these past few weeks, her mother was pushing her away. Celeste was pulling inside herself, struggling alone to find an answer to a problem that Jasmine knew nothing about. Frustration roiled inside her, leaving a bitter taste in her mouth.

As though sensing her distress, Celeste crossed the room and enveloped her in a quick hug. "Don't look so worried, dear. I'll be fine. Go on back to your room. There's no need for both of us to lose any more sleep."

Jasmine had no choice but to comply. Slowly she crossed to the door. Her hand lingering on the knob, she hesitated, glancing back at her mother, watching as Celeste placed a thick candle on the braided rug in the middle of the room. Tucking her nightgown around her, she assumed the lotus position, sitting cross-legged in front of the light. Folding her hands in meditation, she closed her eyes and began to chant beneath her breath.

Feeling like an intruder, Jasmine stepped into the hall and closed the door quietly behind her. As she headed back to her room, a renewed sense of resolve grew inside her, quickening her step.

Since the discovery of Raven Hunter's body, her mother's health and stability had been slowly deteriorating in front of her eyes. Something was troubling Celeste. Something that had to do with the murder of her sister's lover.

She had no doubt Celeste knew something that she wasn't sharing. She'd felt this as certainly as she had felt the tremors shaking her mother's body. But without Celeste confiding in her, Jasmine's hands were tied in her attempts to help her mother.

Which left her with only one choice.

Now there were two reasons to help Storm.

First, in the name of the Kincaid family, she would make amends to him for the wrongs committed against him and his brother. Second, for her mother's sake, she would find out the truth—before it was too late.

Somehow she had to help her mother find peace of mind.

Because, if she didn't, she was afraid that she might lose Celeste for good.

At precisely eleven o'clock the next day, a knock sounded at Storm's hotel room door. Half dressed, his hair still wet and only finger-combed from his shower, he glowered at the closed door. Of all days for Jasmine to be prompt, why did it have to be today?

For the first time in weeks he'd been able to sleep the night through. In fact, he'd slept so soundly, he hadn't heard his alarm. When he finally had awoken and had seen the lateness of the hour, he'd been rushing like a madman ever since.

Growling his impatience, he strode to the door and swung it open.

A smile of greeting died on Jasmine's lips as she skimmed the length of his body, taking in his shirtless, shoeless, blue jeans-clad state. Swallowing hard, she stared at the smooth expanse of his bare chest.

"I'm not ready," he said needlessly.

Raising a thin, dark brow, she quipped, "Isn't that supposed to be a woman's line?"

The tension eased from his muscles at her attempt to lighten the situation. "It'll only take me a few minutes to finish dressing. Would you like to come inside?''

''Mmm...'' She stole another glance at his naked chest and shook her head. ''It's too nice a morning. I'll just wait out here. Take your time.''

He nodded, his lips twitching with the urge to smile as he recalled her bravado of the day before. How she'd assured him there would be no problem with their working together, since she was no longer interested in him in a physical way. It assuaged his bruised ego to know that Jasmine wasn't as immune to him as she'd like for him to believe.

He turned, leaving the door open, and strode to the closet. Pulling out a neatly pressed blue chambray shirt, he slipped it on, tucking the ends into his jeans. Fastening the top button of his fly, he looped a woven belt around his narrow waist and stepped into his shoes.

Glancing outside, he saw Jasmine with her back to him, leaning against a concrete pillar, gazing in the direction of the distant mountains. Her black cowboy boots were crossed at her ankles. She wore a pair of snug blue jeans, coupled with a black scoop-neck T-shirt. The outfit emphasized the flatness of her stomach, the gentle curve of her hips and the primal beauty of her body.

Awareness stirred in Storm, warming his blood, making the fit of his jeans even tighter. He stifled a moan. Jasmine wasn't the only one not immune. The day had barely begun and already his libido was working overtime. He inhaled a steadying breath, releasing it through clenched teeth.

It was going to be a long, long day.

With fierce, punishing strokes, he brushed the hair from his face, tucking it behind his ears. Letting the wet strands air dry, he picked up his keys and headed for the door.

At the sound of his approaching footsteps, Jasmine turned to face him. In the revealing rays of sunlight, he saw for the first time the dark smudges beneath her eyes. He paused in the doorway and frowned his concern. ''You look tired.''

''I didn't sleep well last night.'' Self-consciously she raked both hands through her cropped hair. With a quick smile, she said, ''It was too warm in the house. I couldn't seem to get comfortable.''

Storm didn't believe her for a minute. Jasmine was a terrible liar. There was something she wasn't telling him. He could see that as clearly as the blush of color rising on her cheeks.

He couldn't help but wonder if her restlessness had anything to do with her decision to help him. She had been honest yesterday about her family's wishes for her to not become involved with him. But she'd offered to help him nonetheless. Perhaps the burden of betraying family loyalties was beginning to wear on her.

For his own sake, he hoped not. As hard as it was

to admit, he needed her. There was too much depending upon the success of their mission. He owed his brother the truth. And he didn't have a snowball's chance in hell of uncovering that truth without her.

Closing the door behind him, he joined her on the walkway. Standing close, he experienced the first of what he was sure to be many second thoughts of the day. She looked so fresh, so beautiful. His fingers itched to reach out and touch her. Not trusting himself to indulge his hormonal urges, he crammed his hands into the back pockets of his jeans and wondered how he was going to get through the day without giving in to his desires.

"So, where do we begin?" he asked, unable to keep his eyes off the delicate features of her face.

"The Hip Hop Café," she said. At his look of surprise, she gave a self-deprecating smile. "I made breakfast for our guests this morning at the B and B, but I didn't have time to eat my own. I can't think straight on an empty stomach."

His own smile was obliging. "I guess I could use a cup of coffee, too."

"Good," she said, giving an audible breath of relief. "Without food, in another hour, I'd have been a real bear to live with."

Somehow, he doubted that.

The heel of her boot scraped against the concrete as she turned toward the parking lot. He followed behind her, cutting his long-legged strides to match her smaller steps. But he stayed close enough to be on the receiving end of a heady dose of her sweet-smelling perfume. The scent reminded him of warm, sunny days, of lazing in a meadow surrounded by wildflowers. In the parking lot, she hesitated, glancing between his silver luxury car and her Jeep Wrangler.

"There's no need for both of us to drive," she said, her tone matter-of-fact. "We may be visiting some rugged territory. Four-wheel drive will come in handy. I guess we should take my Jeep."

"Whatever you say," he said, distracted by the way she chewed on her lower lip when trying to work her way through a problem.

Jasmine didn't move. Instead, placing her hands on her hips, she glared at him. "It's not just my decision, Storm. We're supposed to be partners, remember? If you've got an opinion, say so!"

After a moment's consideration he said, "In my opinion, we're wasting time standing here in the parking lot. The daylight's burning. Let's go."

She hesitated. Then, looking as though she'd like to pick up the argument where she'd left off, she gave an impatient humph and strode to her Jeep.

Storm continued at a slower pace. On this warm, cloudless day, she'd driven with the top down. Adjusting the mirrored sunglasses onto the bridge of his nose, he slung himself into the passenger seat and buckled in, adjusting his long legs to the limited space.

Once they were both settled, Jasmine gunned the engine to life. As she popped the car into gear, her long, slender hands caught his eye. Instead of being smooth and manicured, they were red and rough, the nails cut to the quick. They were the hands of a laborer, not of a woman who lived her life at ease.

Curiosity getting the better of him, he asked, "You said you made breakfast this morning?"

"Uh-huh." She turned onto Center Avenue, heading for the café. A brisk wind lifted the short strands of hair from her face. Raising her voice over the noise of the engine, she said, "I make breakfast every day. I'm the chief cook and bottle washer at the B and B. Not too bad at it, either." Her grin was rueful. "At least, that's what I've been told. I guess all that time I spent at culinary school has paid off."

"You're a chef," he said, once again, unable to hide his surprise.

She flashed him an amused glance. "You seem shocked."

"No...well, maybe a little surprised. You don't look—"

"Old enough?" she finished for him. He shifted uncomfortably in his seat as she raised a brow in question. Despite her light tone, he heard the annoyance in her voice when she said, "Don't worry, Storm. Just because I look like a teenybopper, it doesn't mean I live like one."

"That's not what I meant. I—"

"No, I know exactly what you meant. You've got some strange idea in your head that I'm just a kid." Gliding the car into a higher gear, she stomped down on the accelerator. The sudden surge of momentum pushed him back into his seat. She tilted her pert nose skyward, the indignation rising with each word as she said, "Well, you're wrong. I'm twenty-three. Old enough to know what I want to do with my life, and believe it or not, it's being a chef. I've always loved working in the kitchen.

"Learning to hone my skills seemed only logical, since my family owns a bed-and-breakfast." Her brow furrowed. "Actually, I've been trying to talk my mother into expanding the dining room at the B and B, but she's been hesitant about taking on the added responsibility."

She was rambling.

Surprisingly he didn't seem to mind.

Storm normally tuned out the intimate details of the women who'd come and gone in his life. Most of the time he was interested only in surface information such as name, phone number and address. Not to mention how fast he could sneak out once he'd sensed a woman was becoming too interested.

But with Jasmine it was different. He wanted to know all he could about her. Instead of being discomfited by the personal bent of their conversation, he found himself listening carefully, watching the slight pout of her lush lips and the lively sparkle in her eyes as she spoke.

Did she have any idea just how beautiful she really was? She had the finest, most delicate complexion he'd ever seen. Her smooth, flawless skin reminded him of a porcelain doll. But more than just her exotic looks, he was intrigued by what she had to say and how she said it. He'd never met anyone quite like her.

Everything about her seemed to fascinate him.

Braking hard, forcing his thoughts back to the matter at hand, she pulled into the lot of the Hip Hop. Switching off the engine, she turned and looked at him expectantly.

He studied her for a long moment, raising a curious brow. "May I finish what I was about to say now? Or do you have something else to add?"

A flush of pink tinged her cheeks. She waved a dismissive hand. "Go right ahead. Speak your piece."

Biting back an amused smile, he said, "What I was about to say—before I was rudely interrupted—was that I couldn't picture you as a chef because you're so thin. You don't look like a person who spends her time working with food. My surprise had nothing to do with your age, but with your size."

"Oh," she said, her flush deepening. "Sorry, I'm just a little self-conscious about my age. Everyone seems to be pointing out my youthfulness lately. I guess I jumped to the wrong conclusion."

"No apology is necessary," he said, his tone brisk. Reluctantly he glanced at the diner. As usual, it appeared busy. "Should we go inside?"

"Sounds good to me. For once I'd like to put something other than my foot in my mouth."

Storm chuckled. Unbuckling his seat belt, he swung himself out of the Jeep, stepping down onto the paved lot. Still smiling, he held open the door to the café, then stepped inside.

Heads turned, and curious stares bore into them. More than one eyebrow of surprise was raised. Hushed whispers followed their entrance into the restaurant.

And Storm realized their mistake.

Last evening they'd dined at a restaurant owned and operated by a Cheyenne. Not only that, but they'd been accompanied by Gavin and Summer. Their presence together hadn't raised any alarms.

Not so today. Storm wasn't certain if the fact that he was a Native American and Jasmine was white was what had set the town's gossips abuzz. Or if it was the fact that he was a Hunter and she was a Kincaid. Either way, in the town of Whitehorn, the two did not mix.

If Jasmine noticed the extra attention, she gave no outward indication. Instead, with her head held high, her shoulders ramrod straight, she made a beeline for

a pair of empty stools at the front counter. Sliding
onto one, she glanced at him, waiting for him to join
her.

With one last self-conscious glance across the café,
he sat on the vinyl stool.

"What are you having, Storm? The Western ome-
lettes are good," Jasmine said, her light tone sounding forced. She picked up a menu and scanned the
plastic-covered sheet. Lowering her voice, she whispered, "Ignore them, Storm. Whitehorn's a small
town. There's not a lot to do around here. People have
to have something to entertain themselves, even if it
is just finding something to gossip about."

Obviously he'd been wrong. She was fully aware
of the extra attention their entrance had brought.

But she was wrong, too. It did matter what others
thought.

The reaction of the citizens of Whitehorn to their
being together today was the same reaction Raven and
Jasmine's aunt Blanche had received when they were
secret lovers nearly thirty years earlier.

The disapproval in the air was palpable.

Storm's chest tightened with an unwanted emotion.
He didn't want to admit how much it disappointed
him to know that nothing had changed in Whitehorn
since he was just a boy.

Janie, the blond-haired waitress who'd waited on
him the last time he'd dined at the Hip Hop, joined
them at the counter, wearing a contagious grin. "Jas-

mine Monroe, this certainly is a pleasant surprise. It's been a long time since I've seen you in here.''

Jasmine's returning smile was pure mischief. ''Just came to check out the competition, that's all.''

''Well, I'll be sure to tell the cook to be extra careful with your order.'' Her gaze moved from Jasmine to Storm. ''And you brought a friend. It's good to see you again, Mr. Hunter. What can I get for you today?''

''Just coffee, please,'' he said, his somber tone spoiling the lighthearted banter.

''Not too hungry, huh?'' Janie turned to Jasmine. ''How about you, Jasmine? What would you like?''

Sighing, Jasmine placed the menu back in its spot between the sugar and napkin holders. ''Coffee, and one of your special cinnamon rolls. Only could you make both of our orders to go. We're running a little late.''

''Sure thing.'' Janie's smile faltered. She glanced around the café, catching the curious stares of the other patrons. With a quick nod of understanding, she said, ''It'll only be a moment.''

Neither Jasmine nor Storm spoke again until they'd paid for their order and had left the café. Once they were out of earshot of others, only then did he realize just how upset she really was—with him.

She turned on him, anger flashing in her eyes. ''Why did you let them bother you? It doesn't matter what they think about our being together. It doesn't matter what anyone else thinks.''

"Of course it matters,'' he said, his voice harsher than he'd intended. He stopped short, his shoes skidding against a loose rock. The coffee sloshed in his cup, nearly spilling over the brim. Brusquely he added, ''You live here, Jasmine. You need these people's approval.''

She pointed an accusing finger in his direction. Her voice and hand trembling with barely controlled anger, she said, ''Don't you dare tell me what I need. I don't need a watchdog keeping track of my status in the community. I've long given up on the idea of seeking Whitehorn's approval.''

Despite her adamant tone, he heard the pain that underlined the words. A pain that he knew only too well. A pain that came only from a lifetime of shame and guilt.

Somehow, Jasmine had been exposed to the prejudices of others.

Perhaps he'd been too hasty in his assumption of her so-called privileged lifestyle. Perhaps they had more in common than he'd first imagined.

''Jasmine, I'm sorry. I didn't mean to overstep—''

''I don't need your sympathy, Storm,'' she said, cutting off his apology. ''Like you said, daylight's burning. It's time to move on.'' Turning on her heel, she strode to the Jeep.

Reluctantly Storm followed, a burr of discomfort

riding low in his chest. The more he was with Jasmine, the more he learned about her. Before, it was easy to discount her as just one of the Kincaids, the family who'd caused so much pain in his life. Now, his hatred was being replaced with a new and even more disturbing emotion.

Empathy.

Not only did he understand her, but he found himself caring for her, too.

Seven

Wind whistled through the open Jeep, blowing the long, dark strands of hair into Storm's face. Dust boiled up from the tires, covering everything—including himself—with a fine layer of grit. The heavy scent of sage peppered the air as they passed over the rolling green hills of the Kincaid ranch. They'd left the main road a few miles back. Now they were traveling on a hard-packed dirt lane, which would lead them to the original casino/resort construction site.

The site where his brother's remains had been found.

Despite the warm, sunlit day, Storm shivered as a cloud of darkness slowly enveloped him. He knew there was much more to this feeling of dread than having to face the spot where Raven had died. Straight ahead, abutting the Kincaid border, stood the mountains marking the Laughing Horse Reservation—the land that had been his home for the first thirteen years of his life.

Since arriving in Whitehorn, Storm had yet to find a reason, or the will, to visit the place of his birth.

"I doubt if anyone will be at the construction site.

No one's been working there since my cousin Lyle died,'' Jasmine said, raising her voice above the wind, pulling Storm back to the present.

Startled, he glanced her way, thankful for the mirrored sunglasses that hid his eyes.

She continued, seemingly oblivious to the strong emotions churning inside him. "As far as I know, the plans for the casino and resort are on hold. At least until someone can decide what to do next."

Giving himself a moment to collect his thoughts, Storm sipped the last bit of his drink. The dregs of lukewarm coffee tasted bitter. Forcing himself to swallow it down, he said, "I've heard a little about what's happened here, but not the whole story. Do you mind my asking exactly what's been going on at this construction site?"

"No, I don't mind. But the truth is, I'm not really sure if I know the whole story." Shaking her head, she said, "Now that Lyle's dead, I doubt if anyone does. I guess it all started in May, when they broke ground on the resort. Everyone was so excited. There were such high hopes of the venture bringing prosperity to both the reservation and to Whitehorn."

Storm bit the inside of his mouth, resisting the urge to contradict Jasmine's rose-colored view of the real world. From his own experience, he'd found that Native Americans earned prosperity only after leaving the reservation and making their way in the white man's world. For those who stayed on the reservation, prosperity remained an unattainable dream. Too many of his people still lived in poverty, losing all hope of bettering their situations. Even when an opportunity to improve their lives came along, somehow fate always found a way to keep it beyond their grasp.

"As you probably already know, that first site was on Kincaid land. Lyle was appointed by his grandfather, my cousin Garrett, to oversee the family's interest." She paused, taking her eyes off the road long enough to send him a hesitant glance. "It wasn't long after they broke ground that they discovered your brother's remains."

Storm schooled himself to show no reaction, unwilling to let her see the depth of his own pain.

Despite his efforts to remain aloof, concern flickered in her eyes. He hadn't fooled her for a moment. Despite her uncertainty, Jasmine continued, "Instead of delaying the construction, they moved the site. All was going well until Peter Cook, one of the workers, was killed. One morning they found his body at the bottom of the construction pit. At first everyone thought it was an accident. But there were signs of a struggle, and it was decided that he'd been murdered. Apparently he'd been pushed to his death." She stopped and shuddered, looking sickened by the horrible events she'd just relayed.

Storm remained silent, not sure how to respond to her obvious distress. Though he wanted to reach out and comfort her, he didn't know if the overture would be welcome, or wise. He'd made that mistake earlier, when he'd tried to convince her that she needed Whitehorn's approval.

Theirs was a temporary relationship of convenience, he reminded himself. As soon as his brother's murder was solved, he'd be on the first flight back to New Mexico. No matter how tempting it might be, for his own sake, as well as hers, it would be best to not become too involved in Jasmine's life.

After a moment she said, "Gretchen Neal—she's the detective handling the case—"

"I've met Ms. Neal," he said, his voice sharper than he'd intended. His dealings with the detective and her FBI partner David Hannon, Jasmine's own cousin, had been frustrating, to say the least. The two had seemed more intent on solving the murder of the white man, Peter Cook, than on finding the truth behind his brother's death.

Not that he should have been surprised. It had been Storm's experience that the concerns of a white man always took priority over those of an Indian's.

Jasmine's gaze lingered on his face, as though she had read his thoughts. Finally she said, "Then you know that Gretchen discovered evidence linking Lyle to Peter Cook's murder."

Storm nodded.

Reluctantly she turned her gaze back to the road. "That's why we think Lyle tried to kill her. To silence her. Thankfully, David was able to stop him before he succeeded.''

Storm mulled this over, then asked, ''Does anyone know why Lyle murdered Peter Cook?''

''Not that I've heard. His grandfather and his parents were stunned by Lyle's actions. They haven't a clue what could have triggered such bizarre behavior.''

He studied her face, seeing the telltale doubts in her expression. ''How about you? Do you have any idea why Lyle might have done something like this?''

She hesitated a moment before answering. Grimacing, she said, ''Lyle was a distant cousin of mine. He lived in Elk Springs most of his life, so we really didn't see much of each other. But what I did know of him, I didn't like. He was mean-spirited and spoiled, always looking for the easy way to make fast money.'' The sound of her resigned sigh carried on the wind. ''If I had to guess, I'd say that greed motivated him.''

''Greed?'' Storm frowned. ''I don't understand. I thought Garrett Kincaid owned the land the resort's being built on.''

''He does,'' Jasmine said. ''That's what makes it all the more confusing. Lyle tried to buy the land from Garrett a few weeks ago. But Garrett refused to sell it, he wanted the land to go to Gabriel Reilly Baxter, his youngest grandson. Now no one can figure out what Lyle hoped to gain by killing Peter Cook.

But I'd bet my favorite saucepan there was something he was hiding, something that would have made him a rich man. The problem is, now that both Lyle and Peter Cook are dead, no one ever will know the truth.''

History did have a way of repeating itself, Storm mused with an unexpected tinge of bitterness. In his heart he believed that Jasmine's uncle, Jeremiah Kincaid, was responsible for his brother's death. But both Jeremiah and Raven were now dead. The truth behind what had really happened thirty years ago on the night Raven died may be buried along with them. This trip to uncover the past may just be a waste of their time.

Jasmine shifted gears, slowing the Jeep.

Up ahead was the abandoned construction site. Dust devils danced across the barren landscape. Sunlight shimmered off the surface that had been stripped of its topsoil. Heavy machinery stood in silent testimony to the tragedy that had taken place on this site. Like a dark plague, desolation and despair hovered in the air.

It was the first time Storm had visited the site where his brother had supposedly died. A fist of dread gripped his chest, making it hard for him to breathe. He took a shallow breath, struggling to calm his nerves.

Bypassing the newer construction pit, Jasmine slowly steered the Jeep toward the original site. There in the distance Storm saw the yellow crime scene tape rippling in the wind, marking the spot where Raven's remains had been found. His pulse quickened. He steeled himself against the ribbon of pain that flowed through him.

Before he was ready to face the past, Jasmine coasted the Jeep to a stop.

A stifling blanket of dust caught up with them, rolling over them like a thick, dark cloud. Grit coated his skin, clung to his face, his lashes. His eyes burned in irritation—or with emotion, he wasn't sure which.

Jasmine switched off the engine, but remained in her seat. She turned to look at him, waiting for him to take the first step.

Unable to move, he sat frozen in his seat, staring straight ahead.

"Storm?" she asked, her voice tentative, gentle. "Are you sure you want to do this? You don't have to be here—"

"Yes, I do," Storm said, suddenly finding his voice. "This is where my brother's body lay for thirty years. I owe it to Raven to see where he died."

Taking a deep breath of courage, Storm stepped out of the Jeep. His feet felt leaden as he moved slowly toward the area cordoned off by the yellow tape. Behind him he heard the scrape of a boot against the hard-packed dusty ground. Prickles of awareness feathered his skin, telling him that Jasmine was close.

Encouraged by her presence, he forced himself to continue. He ducked beneath the crime scene tape, holding it up for Jasmine to pass under. Her black T-shirt was covered with a thin layer of dust. Her short hair was mussed by the wind, and by restless fingers plowing through it. Deep lines of tension etched her face. She looked almost as nervous as he felt.

But still she found the strength to give him a smile and an encouraging nod.

The shallow pit of an abandoned foundation lay in the center of the circle of tape. Scrape marks from a hand shovel identified the exact location where his brother's remains had been excavated. Removing his sunglasses, Storm tucked them into the breast pocket of his shirt and carefully made his way to the spot.

Jasmine stood close at his side as he lowered himself on bent knee. Holding his hand inches above the ground, he let it hover for a moment. Saying a silent prayer for the spirits to guide him in his quest to allow his brother's soul to finally find rest, he closed his eyes and lowered his hand to the ground, raking his fingers through the powdery dust.

And felt nothing but a vast emptiness in his heart.

Storm's brows knitted into a frown. His eyes shot open. He scooped up a handful of dirt, letting it sift slowly through his long fingers. Then, shaking the dust from his hand, he looked up, meeting Jasmine's confused gaze.

"My brother's remains may have been here, but his soul never was. He died elsewhere."

* * *

"We need to tell the police," Jasmine insisted, quickening her step to catch up with Storm's long-legged stride to the Jeep, unable to shake the feeling that he was running away.

His strong jaw set in a resolute line, he remained stubbornly silent, refusing to answer.

Frustrated at being ignored, she grabbed his arm.

He stopped, wheeling around to face her. His eyes were dark, his glare forbidding. Beneath her fingers she felt a slight tremor in the powerful, sinewy muscles of his forearm, as though he were struggling for control.

A twinge of unwanted fear riffled through her. She tightened her grip, determined to not back down, or to let him see the effect he had on her. "We should let Gretchen Neal know that Raven was killed elsewhere. It could send the investigation into a more positive direction."

Silently, deliberately, Storm looked down at her hand. Then he raised his eyes to her face. She shivered as he held her in his gaze for a long, discomfiting moment. Finally he said, "We can't do that. We can't go to the police."

"Why not?"

"Because, Jasmine, no matter how good a detective she might be, Ms. Neal won't be willing to change the course of her investigation simply because of a 'feeling.' Especially if she knew that feeling came from someone like me, an Indian."

Disappointment and anger billowed up inside Jasmine at the unjustness of his statement. With an irritated breath, she released him, dropping her hand to her side. In his own way Storm was just as narrow-minded as the rest of the people of Whitehorn. She opened her mouth, ready to argue that his heritage should not stand in the way of Gretchen listening to him.

But something stopped her.

Reason returned.

She, of all people, should understand the prejudices of others. She'd grown up with her mother, Celeste, a woman who'd done nothing to hide her beliefs in the spiritual hereafter. Over the years Jasmine had endured the ridicule of a town that thought of her mother as an oddity. But it had not been easy. Unfortunately she understood Storm's hesitancy in revealing his "feelings" to a complete stranger.

With a resigned sigh, the last of her anger dissolved. "All right, we can't talk to the police...yet. So what should we do next?"

"There's nothing more we can accomplish here," he said as he glanced around the construction site. His impatient gaze glided over the dusty barren ground, the abandoned machinery and the gaping pit. He shook his head, his frustration obvious. "I just keep wondering if there's a connection between finding Raven's remains and Lyle's unexplained behavior. If only we could talk to someone who knew Lyle best. Someone who might be able to help us understand what he had on his mind before he started his rampage.''

Jasmine frowned, considering the problem. "Lyle was closest to his mother. Even if she would talk to us, which I doubt, she's already gone back to Elk Springs."

"What about Lyle's grandfather?"

"Garrett?" She shrugged, considering the possibility. "He did spend a lot of time with Lyle those last few weeks."

"Do you think he would talk to us?"

"He's always seemed like a fair and honest man to me. But there's only one way to find out for sure. Why don't we pay him a visit?"

Storm nodded. "Let's go."

Her step lighter, more purposeful, Jasmine headed for the Jeep, chattering as she did so. "Garrett's been living at the main house since he moved to Whitehorn. Right now we're at the opposite end of the Kincaid ranch. I know of a shortcut, though. It'll be quicker if we go through the reservation to get back onto the main road."

Storm's step faltered.

Jasmine skidded on the sandy soil, forcing herself to stop. She looked at him, unable to hide her concern. "Is something wrong?"

"No, nothing's wrong," he said, his tone curt. Once again a stony mask of indifference slipped into place, hiding the flicker of emotion. "It's just this site... It's giving me the creeps. The sooner we get out of here, the better."

Jasmine nodded and continued walking, but she didn't believe Storm's explanation for a second. She'd seen the look in his eyes. His sudden wariness had nothing to do with the construction site. He hadn't acted skittish until she'd mentioned the reservation.

Unbidden, she felt a surge of sympathy for him. Storm seemed so lost, reminding her of a drifting soul. Though he'd reached out to Summer, the only other time he'd mentioned his family was in regard to Raven's death. She had no idea if he still had any other ties to Laughing Horse.

If his reaction to going back to the reservation was any indication, she doubted it.

Pushing aside the troubling thought, she climbed into the Jeep and waited for Storm to join her. Once he was settled, she revved the engine to life. Making a quick U-turn, she headed down the gravel road that would take them to the reservation.

The road soon narrowed, rising and falling as they skirted the foothills of the Crazy Mountains. With the aid of the four-wheel drive, Jasmine maneuvered the Jeep through the rugged terrain with ease, seeming to enjoy the bumpy ride.

Storm glanced at her, his brow raised in question

as she plowed through a shallow creek bed and sent a spray of water shooting up into the air around them. "Are you sure you know where you're going?"

She grinned. "You're not worried, are you?"

"Worried? Of course not. We're only miles from nowhere. No living soul in sight. It's just the spot I'd pick to have a flat tire, or a breakdown."

"So much for your confidence in my driving abilities," she said, raising her nose in indignation. But he caught the twinkle in her eye and the slight curve of a smile on her lips.

Her lighthearted mood worked to ease some of the tension from his muscles. The truth was, Storm had never intended to return to Laughing Horse. Now that he was on reservation land, he tried to ignore the growing sense of dread.

"I'll have you know I've spent many a summer exploring these mountains," she said, interrupting his pensive thoughts. "I know these peaks like the back of my hand. Besides, we're not that far from civilization."

As though to prove her point, the ground slowly leveled out. The road, while still rugged, straightened, with tall, fragrant stands of pine trees flanking both sides. While he knew the effort was futile, he sat back and tried to not let disturbing memories interfere with his enjoyment of the breathtaking scenery.

He glanced at Jasmine. "Do you mind if I ask you something?"

"Not at all. Ask away," she said, keeping her tone light, though he heard the catch of uncertainty in her voice.

Earlier he'd warned himself to keep a safe distance from her. Now he was breaking his own silent vow to not become personally involved. But he felt the need to find something—anything—to keep his mind off of his own past.

"Back at the construction site, when I told you that Raven died elsewhere, you accepted my feeling without question. I just wondered why."

"Years of experience," Jasmine said with a self-deprecating smile. Then she explained. "I grew up with a mother who places a lot of stock in the power of the spiritual hereafter. Communicating with restless souls from the past is an everyday occurrence in my household."

"Your mother communicates with the dead?" Storm frowned, not sure whether to believe her.

"Seances, meditation…you name it, she does it."

"I see."

"No, I don't think you do. I know it sounds crazy," she said, her tone defensive. "But I've witnessed too many things to know that not everything my mother believes in can be attributed to what people call 'a high-strung woman's overactive imagination.'"

"I never said I didn't believe you," he said, meeting her fiery gaze. "Respecting your mother's faith in the spiritual world isn't crazy. It only proves that you're wise for someone so young."

"Here we go again with my age." She shook her head and rolled her eyes. "You know, it's funny, but my mother used to tell me that I was old beyond my years. She called me an 'old soul' and insisted that a part of me lived before in another life."

Storm didn't laugh at her mother's homegrown explanation. Instead he said, "The Cheyenne hold similar beliefs and explanations for the unknown. Your mother has good instincts despite..." He stopped, letting the words drift.

"Despite the way she's behaved since you've arrived in town?" Jasmine finished for him. Sighing, she said, "Believe it or not, my mother is one of the most open-minded people I've ever known. Her reaction to you has been unusual. Never before has she allowed the color of a man's skin or his family heritage to influence her judgment of him."

"I believe you, Jasmine," he said, surprising himself that he really meant the soothing words. "This investigation into my brother's death has been difficult for all of us. I know it's placed a strain on your mother. I, of all people, should know what stress can do to a person."

She looked at him, her gaze questioning.

Knowing he'd said too much, but unable to stop, he purged himself of memories that had been bottled up inside him for too many years. "When I left Laughing Horse I was only thirteen years old."

"You were just a boy."

Storm shook his head. "I hadn't been a boy for many years. I was old enough to fend for myself. For a long time, I wandered until I found a place in New Mexico to settle. I worked during the day on a ranch. At night, I studied to earn my high school degree. From there, I went on to Albuquerque and attended college, then law school."

"You've accomplished a lot in your lifetime," she said, her voice tentative.

"If you mean by accumulating material wealth, yes, I have. Over the years I've worked hard to succeed in the white man's world." He looked out at the beautiful landscape of the Laughing Horse Reservation. "But in the eyes of the Cheyenne, material items aren't what's important. The richest man on the reservation is the man who gives of himself to everyone else. Despite the pro bono work and the civil liberty cases that I've taken on to defend my people, I've traveled among the white man for so long, I've forgotten my own roots. The years have made my heart hard."

"I'm sorry, Storm. I had no idea—"

"I'm not looking for sympathy, Jasmine," he said, cutting her off abruptly. "I only meant to tell you that I understand how your mother must feel. That I know of the burden of responsibility that we place upon ourselves."

Emotion shimmered in her eyes. Jasmine looked as though she wanted to say something more to ease his turmoil. But she hesitated, looking uncertain. Instead she let the silence lengthen between them and focused her attention on the rugged road.

Soon a homestead came into view. The paint on the white clapboard house was peeling. Chickens roamed the grounds, scratching in the dirt. To one side of the yard, a car was raised on cement blocks, its wheels missing.

Storm replaced his sunglasses and he pressed his lips into a grim line as he fought to control the anxiety mounting inside him. They passed more houses, each in various states of disrepair. As they neared the heart of the reservation, Storm held himself stiffly in his seat. Unable to help himself, he searched the streets for a familiar landmark.

Then suddenly it was there.

"Stop," he said, startling Jasmine. He pointed to a small, ramshackle house. "Pull over there."

Braking, Jasmine did as he'd asked. She slid the Jeep to a stop at the side of the road, parking next to a thick tangle of weeds and overgrown grass. Turning off the engine, she swiveled around to face him, watching him as he stared at the house.

It looked abandoned, in even worse shape than the others they'd passed. Rusting junk filled the untended yard. The small shack leaned unsteadily on its foundation. The paint was completely worn from its clapboard siding. The collapsed remains of a front porch lay on the ground, as though no one had bothered to pick it up from where it had fallen. Sadly, the neglected house looked beyond repair.

Sliding his sunglasses from the bridge of his nose, Storm studied the abandoned house, his eyes stinging with unwanted emotion. He slung himself out of the Jeep. Unmindful of the brambly weeds that snagged his jeans, he took a step toward the house. Then stopped. Standing frozen in the yard, he stared in silence.

Climbing down from the Jeep, swishing her way through the tall weeds, Jasmine joined him. She stood quietly beside him, waiting for him to speak.

"This was my parents' house," he said, finally finding his voice, though the words sounded flat, hollow of emotion. "This is where I spent the first thirteen years of my life."

Jasmine didn't say a word. Not pushing him, she let him decide how much to reveal.

"My parents were alcoholics," he said, unable to stop the words, needing to share his past with her. "For as long as I remember, my father went from one job to another, never finding anything that would satisfy him. My mother grew tired of complaining. She gave up on changing his ways. Instead of trying to improve their lives, they both turned to alcohol to escape their fate.''

He swallowed hard as the bitter taste of self-pity rose in his throat. ''My brother, Raven, was older than me. He was more of a father to me than my own father ever was. As long as Raven was here, life was bearable. But when he left...'' He shook his head, closing his eyes against the painful memory. ''I couldn't stand to live here any longer. When Raven left, I ran away, and I didn't look back.''

Her voice gentle, she asked, ''You never heard from your parents?''

Opening his eyes, he forced himself to look at the house that still haunted his dreams. His throat tightening, he said, ''No, no one ever tried to find me. If they even noticed that I was gone, they were probably relieved that I'd left. It was one less mouth for them to feed.''

''Oh, Storm,'' she murmured, her voice catching with emotion. ''I'm so sorry.''

Giving a mirthless laugh, he said, ''So am I.''

Until that moment Jasmine had kept her distance, letting him spill out all of his anger and bitterness. Now she did the one thing he needed the most—she reached out and took him into her arms. With her warm, reassuring body pressed against his, she held him close until the tremors shaking his body were stilled.

Eight

The bond between them was growing stronger.

In front of the deserted home of his youth, Jasmine held Storm in her arms, not afraid to give him the comfort she instinctively knew he needed. He clung to her, his large hands gripping her waist, holding her tight. His strong body trembled, overwhelmed by emotions to which only he was privy. With a sigh, he pressed his smooth cheek against hers. Their bodies melded and she felt his heart pounding in his chest, matching her own erratic pulse beat for beat. Their stolen moment of closeness brought a quivering of awareness deep in the pit of her belly.

She wasn't sure how long they stood that way, entwined in each other's arms. Time seemed to have stopped. It had no meaning, no consequences. All that mattered was holding him, touching him, easing his pain.

His chest rose and fell as he took in a deep breath. Still holding her close, he lifted his head, just far enough to look at her. With her face inches from his, their lips almost touching, the air crackled between them with a sensual spark of awareness. Heat flushed her skin. Her breath caught in her throat. In his dark eyes, she saw the reflection of her own desire.

Slowly, Storm lowered his head, closing the distance between them. He came closer…and closer… until the shadow of a large, dark bird passed overhead, blocking the sun. Swooping low, it landed in a nearby tree, disturbing a squirrel from its branch. The rodent's chattering protest echoed across the yard, spoiling the quiet hush that had surrounded them.

Distracted, Storm glanced up at the tree and frowned.

Jasmine felt a twinge of disappointment at the interruption. Her lips longed for his touch. Her body throbbed with a need only Storm could fulfill. She had never felt this way before, this restless ache deep inside her. It seemed incomprehensible that the world around her had remained unchanged while her life had been turned upside down. In her heart she knew nothing would ever be the same.

But it was more than just lust. Whether Storm wanted to admit it or not, they were connecting on a level that went beyond a mere physical attraction. Though they'd met each other only a short time ago, it seemed as though she'd known him all her life. She shivered, struck once again by a feeling of déjà vu. The ease they felt when they were together, the undeniable attraction that raged just below the surface, it was as though they'd been lovers once before.

That they were meant to be together again.

Curling her fingers into the thick strands of hair at the back of his neck, she forced his attention back to her. Her resolve melted beneath the sudden intensity of his troubled gaze. Gathering her strength, she said, "Storm, I—"

Before she could put into words what she felt in her heart, a truck slowly drove past, its driver staring at them. Jasmine recognized the driver. He was the reservation's new tribal chief, Jackson Hawk.

She wasn't the only one to notice the unexpected attention.

Storm's muscles tensing, he looked across the yard to meet the other man's curious gaze.

Though it was obvious the two men knew each other, instead of stopping, Jackson Hawk continued down the gravel road. Storm's reaction was quick and brutal. He pushed himself from her embrace. With a look of chagrin, he put an unforgivable distance between them.

Jasmine felt a chill that had nothing to do with the warm weather. The coldness came from within, from the icy fear that had enveloped her heart.

"It's getting late," Storm said, his voice as distant as the look now in his eyes. "If we're going to the Kincaid ranch to visit Garrett, we'd better get moving."

Numbly, Jasmine nodded. Her vision blurred with unwanted tears as she waded through the tall weeds.

Blinking hard, she refused to let her own disappointment show. She would not allow Storm to see just how much she'd been hurt by his rejection. Obviously she'd been wrong. She'd read more into the embrace than Storm had meant.

The heavier sound of his footsteps followed her to the Jeep. Jasmine's heart thumped so hard against her chest, she thought it might break in two. Never before had she felt such pain.

Over and over again in her mind's eye, she saw the stony expression cross Storm's face when Jackson Hawk had driven by, the quickness with which he'd pushed her away. A part of her couldn't help but wonder if Storm was embarrassed at being caught in an intimate embrace with her because she wasn't a Native American, if in his own way, he held a prejudice against the color of her skin.

Unsettled by the thought, Jasmine climbed into the Jeep and waited for him to join her. She refused to look at him, keeping her gaze focused on her trembling hands that she held fisted in her lap.

Storm approached. He hesitated, standing with one hand braced against the rollover bar, watching her. With a prickling of awareness, she felt the heavy measure of his gaze. He didn't move, or speak, until she raised her eyes to look at him. "Jasmine, I..." He stopped, averted his gaze and swore softly beneath his breath. Then facing her once again, he said, "I just wanted to thank you. Coming here today...it wasn't easy for me. I appreciate not having to be alone.''

She nodded, feeling a sudden rush of warmth. The icy lock thawed from around her heart. He'd neither apologized nor explained his behavior. But his gratitude was a step in the right direction. For now it would have to do.

"You're welcome, Storm," she said, hiding her relief behind a crisp, business-like tone. "Now, I'd like to get to the Kincaid ranch before it gets too late."

"Yes, ma'am." The corner of his mouth lifted into a half grin, softening the hard angles of his face. With a mock salute, he climbed aboard, settling his tall frame into the seat next to hers.

Jasmine turned the ignition and revved the motor to life. Pulling away from the grassy roadside, she drove from the house that held so many bittersweet memories for Storm, thankful to be leaving it behind.

The rest of their journey through the Laughing Horse Reservation was accomplished in uneasy silence. Though they received a handful of stares from curious passersby, no one stopped to wave or to make them feel welcome. Glad to escape the unwanted scrutiny, Jasmine turned onto the main road and headed for the Kincaid ranch.

The sun lit the grounds of the ranch house. A cool breeze swept the manicured yard of the stately surroundings. But there wasn't a single soul in sight. Jasmine wondered if they should have called before stopping by. She hoped they hadn't wasted their time, making the long trip.

Parking in front of the house, Jasmine smoothed a hand through her wind-tousled hair and stepped out of the Jeep. She waited for Storm to join her on the front steps. Standing in front of the house, she felt goose bumps race across her skin as an omen of dread traveled through her.

If she was this nervous at the thought of entering the ranch house, she wondered what Storm must be feeling. After all, this was the house where Storm's brother, Raven, and her aunt, Blanche, had met and had fallen in love. Tragically, it was also the last place Raven had been seen alive.

Despite the dark history the house held for both of their families, Storm seemed amazingly at ease. He walked with confidence, his head held high and his wide shoulders straight. It was as though he were trying to prove a point to anyone who might be watching. That no one would take away his pride.

Giving Storm a quick smile of encouragement, Jasmine rang the doorbell.

Garrett Kincaid answered the door himself, much to her surprise. Tall and rawboned, in his early seventies, Garrett had a thick head of silvery hair. Standing in the doorway of the sprawling ranch house, his resemblance to Jeremiah Kincaid was uncanny. It was as though the family photos of Jeremiah had come to life. So taken aback by this unexpected image of her late uncle, Jasmine found herself speechless.

The similarity ended when, instead of receiving her uncle's usual scowl, Garrett smiled in greeting. Jeremiah would never have been quite so civil to an unexpected guest. "Jasmine, this is a surprise. And you've brought a visitor. Please come in, both of you."

Stepping back, he let them enter the large foyer.

The spacious rooms were cool and dark. The furnishings in the house looked well-worn and dated, but still comfortable.

Remembering her manners, Jasmine turned to Garrett, making the proper introductions. "Garrett, I'd like you to meet Storm Hunter. Storm, Garrett Kincaid."

The two men shook hands. Of similar height and build, they stood eye-to-eye, sizing each other up. Unlike her mother, or the townspeople of Whitehorn, Garrett didn't question her being in Storm's company. His instant acceptance shouldn't have surprised her, since he shared Storm's heritage. Cheyenne blood also ran through Garrett's veins.

"Hunter?" Garrett frowned, his gaze thoughtful. "The name sounds familiar. You wouldn't be related to—"

"Raven Hunter," Storm finished for him. "He was my brother."

Garrett nodded, the news bringing a flicker of concern to his eyes. "I see."

"That's why we're here," Jasmine said, hurrying to explain. "The investigation into Raven's death is going nowhere. We're trying to find any new information that might help us figure out what happened on the night he died."

Garrett lifted one silvery brow. "I've already talked to the police when they came to check Jeremiah's old gun collection. I'm not sure what else I can add."

"This ranch, it's where—" Storm stopped, looking frustrated.

"It's where Raven was last seen alive," Jasmine finished for him. "And the construction site for the casino and resort, it's where Raven's remains were found. We know your connection to Raven's death is secondhand, but there's still a connection."

"I guess I see your point." Garrett sighed. "Well, let's not stand here in the foyer. Let's go to the study, where it's more comfortable, and talk about this."

The study was large and roomy, the furniture masculine. Bookcases and faded wallpaper lined the walls. The deep hues of an Oriental rug covered the polished wooden floor. A large desk stood in the center of the room, with a worn leather chair behind it, and a pair of matching wing chairs in front. Garrett stepped behind the desk, taking his place in the leather swivel chair. Jasmine and Storm claimed the wing chairs for themselves.

"Now," Garrett said, the leather creaking as he turned his chair toward them, "how can I help you?"

Jasmine glanced at Storm, looking to him for guidance. Instead of meeting her gaze, he gripped the arms of his chair and stared straight ahead. Since Garrett was her relative, she assumed that he wanted her to do the questioning. Turning to Garrett, she said, "We just came from the construction site for the casino and resort, the place where Raven's remains were found."

Garrett nodded, encouraging her to continue.

Storm remained unusually quiet.

"It's just that, we feel the coincidence is odd. Raven's body being found at the construction site, then Lyle doing what he did. We can't help but wonder if there's a connection between Raven's death and Lyle's—" She stopped, biting her lip. "Well, his unexpected behavior."

"You don't have to sugarcoat it for my sake, Jasmine," Garrett said with a weary sigh. "Lyle went off the deep end. He killed one person and tried to murder another. His behavior was more than unexpected. It was unforgivable."

Jasmine flushed, feeling as though she were invading Garrett's private grief. "I'm sorry, Garrett. I know how hard this must be. Maybe we shouldn't be here now."

"No," Garrett said, giving his head a firm shake. "I'm glad you came. Everyone else has been pussy-footing around, treating me like I was as fragile as an eggshell. It feels good to talk about it, to get it out in the open." He leaned back in his chair and frowned. "The problem is, I don't see how there could be a connection between Lyle's and Raven's deaths." He looked at Storm. "From what I understand, your brother apparently died almost thirty years ago."

Storm nodded.

Jasmine glanced at him, her concern growing. Something was wrong. Storm was more than just quiet. His face had taken on an unhealthy pallor. Fine droplets of sweat beaded his forehead. His jaw was clenched in a tight line. He looked as though he'd been strickened.

"Well, Lyle was only twenty-two," Garrett continued, oblivious to the undercurrents of tension flowing through the room. "He wasn't even born when Raven died."

"I know it sounds crazy," Jasmine said, forcing herself to concentrate on the conversation at hand. "But somehow it seems as though finding Raven's remains triggered the events leading to Lyle's death. Did Lyle say anything to you that might have explained his strange behavior?"

"Not to me," Garrett said, his tone regretful. "Other than complaining about the delay in construction, Lyle never talked about the discovery of Raven Hunter's remains.''

Jasmine gave a frustrated sigh, unwilling to admit they were wasting their time. ''So what happens next? The construction site looked abandoned. With all the bad luck surrounding the site, I wouldn't blame you if you decided to scrap the plans.''

''The plans haven't been scrapped,'' Garrett said, his voice ringing with determination. ''In fact, I've just been talking to the tribal leaders at Laughing Horse. We've decided to go ahead with the casino and resort. But this time I'll be taking over the Kincaid interests. I'm going to make damned sure that a fair arrangement is made with the Cheyenne people.''

Jasmine felt a new respect for the older man. She wondered how a man with such strength and morality could have spawned a grandchild as corrupt and evil as Lyle had been. ''Will you be starting soon?''

''Just as soon as the engineers pick another site for us to dig on.'' Shaking his head, he gave a wry grin. ''Can you believe it? We hit a stubborn vein of bedrock at the second site. Now we have to move the whole shebang and start all over again.''

Jasmine shivered. ''More bad luck.''

''That's for sure,'' Garrett said, his sigh wistful. Suddenly he seemed very tired, the years showing on his face.

Sensing that they'd overstayed their welcome, Jasmine stood. Storm followed her lead, rising slowly to his feet, his expression still troubled.

Garrett rounded the desk and escorted them through the house to the front door. Turning to Storm, he extended a hand and said, "Good luck with your search. I hope you'll find what you've been looking for soon."

"Thank you for your help," Storm said, accepting the polite gesture, seeming to have regained some of his composure.

Garrett enveloped Jasmine in a bear hug and murmured, "It's good to see you again, Jasmine. Next time bring the rest of your family along and we'll have a proper visit."

She nodded an assent and smiled. Exchanging their good-byes, Jasmine and Storm returned to the Jeep and left the Kincaid ranch. But before they'd even gotten past the front gates, Storm leaned back in his seat, closed his eyes and took an audible breath.

Jasmine shot him a worried glance and demanded, "What's wrong?"

"Nothing," he said, shaking his head. Slowly he opened his eyes, though he wouldn't meet her gaze. "Just the beginnings of a headache."

She frowned, not sure whether to believe him. Storm didn't look like the type of man who let something as small as a headache stand in the way of his getting what he wanted. "You didn't say much in Garrett's study."

"You were asking all the right questions. I didn't see the need to interfere."

"Interfere? Storm, this is your brother's death we're looking into. You, of all people, should have the right to ask a few simple questions."

He sighed, looking out onto the late day sun along the horizon of the rolling expanse of green pastures. "What Garrett had to say...that wasn't what was most important about our visit to the Kincaid ranch."

"It wasn't?" Her frown deepened. "Then what was this all about? Why did we go out of our way to get here, if it wasn't to talk to Garrett?"

"The house, Jasmine," he said cryptically. "The answer is in the house."

Jasmine gripped the steering wheel, feeling the frustration churning inside her. "I don't understand. What does the house have to do with anything?"

He shook his head. "I'm not sure, yet. But there's something."

"Storm, you're not making any sense."

"I know," he said, rubbing a hand to his temple, looking tired and beaten. "Trust me, Jasmine. I'm just as confused as you are. As soon as I figure it out, you'll be the first person I'll tell."

This time she did believe him. At the moment Storm was being deliberately evasive, but perhaps with good reason. Something obviously had bothered him when he was in the study at the Kincaid ranch.

But if he didn't want to share his unease with her, then she must respect his wishes.

Besides, he'd promised to tell her the truth eventually. It was time to prove that she trusted his word.

They drove the rest of the way into town in silence. When they arrived at Storm's hotel, Jasmine parked the Jeep in a slot in front of his room. Delaying his departure, she shifted in her seat to look at him. ''That headache of yours any better?''

He grimaced. ''Not much.''

''It's getting late. Neither of us has had much to eat today. Maybe dinner would help?''

His gaze lingered on her face. He looked tempted by the offer. ''Dinner sounds good. Unfortunately, I'm just not up to it right now. Do you mind if I take a rain check?''

''Of course not,'' she said, averting her gaze, feeling the telltale warmth of embarrassment rise on her face. Being turned down wasn't easy, no matter what the circumstance.

''Jasmine,'' he said, his voice a hoarse whisper against the softness of the dusky hour. Before she realized his intentions, Storm reached across the car, crooking his fingers beneath her chin. He lifted her face to look at him. ''Thank you for helping me today.''

She swallowed hard, not trusting herself to answer.

But she didn't need to speak.

Storm's actions spoke volumes, needing little interpretation. Leaning across the seat, he tenderly captured her mouth with his.

Jasmine's lips trembled beneath his gentle kiss. Closing her eyes, she took in a shuddering breath, savoring the feel of his warm mouth against hers.

Seeming encouraged by her response, Storm slid his hand to the back of her neck, cradling her. Slowly, deliberately, he pulled her closer and deepened the kiss.

She gripped his shoulders, steadying herself, giving in to the sweet sensations that flooded her body. Moist heat pooled in the pit of her stomach, sending out warm tendrils of awareness. Never before had she felt such an intense longing for a man. Yet these new feelings didn't scare her. Touching him, kissing him, wanting him, it all seemed as natural as taking a breath.

Tentatively, his tongue brushed her lips.

Without hesitation, she opened her mouth to his gentle demands. Twining her fingers through his thick strands of hair, she tugged him even closer.

Moaning, he glided his hands down the length of her back. His long fingers spanned her waist, measuring its narrow breadth. The heat of his palms burned through the thin material of her shirt, branding her with his touch.

Her strength abandoned her. Jasmine collapsed against him, losing all sense of caution and reason in the smoky haze of desire.

Impatiently he shifted his long legs, angling for a more comfortable position. In the process, he knocked his knee against the gearshift. The crack of bone against the metal bar sounded in the Jeep, splintering the intimate mood, bringing them both crashing back to reality.

Reluctantly Jasmine pushed away, giving herself a much-needed moment to cool her passion-heated senses.

What had she been thinking?

They were in the middle of a hotel parking lot, teetering on the verge of making love, their actions exposed for anyone to see. In a town the size of Whitehorn, gossip traveled fast. While she didn't care about what others thought, she did care about her mother. Celeste didn't know Jasmine had spent the day with Storm. All it would take was a simple phone call from a concerned "friend" for Celeste to know her daughter had lied to her once again.

"I need to go," she said, with all the regret she felt in her heart.

Storm nodded, studying her flushed face. "We have a lot to talk about. When can I see you again?"

"Tomorrow," she promised as his words raised the fine hairs on the back of her neck, signaling a reckless thrill of excitement. This time he'd made no pretense of using the hunt for Raven's murderer as an excuse to see her. They were skirting dangerous territory. "Late morning, after breakfast at the B and B."

Storm nodded. With one last lingering look, he climbed out onto the pavement. Standing on the sidewalk, he watched as she started the engine and backed out of the parking lot.

With his gaze following her, Jasmine felt his presence as though he were still sitting next to her. She had never felt this way before, this overwhelmed by a man.

Little by little, Storm was letting down his defenses. They were getting closer by the minute. While encouraged, she tried not to let her hopes get too high, or to read too much into his actions.

In her heart she knew they were meant to be together. Today they'd taken a giant step toward forging a real relationship. But there were still too many obstacles standing in their way. Only time would tell if they could make this fledgling alliance last.

Storm stood outside his hotel room and watched until the tail lights of the Jeep faded into the dusky twilight. His heart beat so fast against his rib cage it felt as though it were about to explode. His lungs burned in his chest. Slowly he released the breath he hadn't even realized he'd been holding.

She'd gotten to him somehow.

Despite his resolve to keep her at arm's length, Jasmine had done what no other woman had ever accomplished. She'd broken through that protective shell he'd carefully erected around his heart. And she'd made him care.

Care about the future.

Care about her.

He hadn't a clue what to do next.

Storm raked both hands through his hair, tucking the long strands behind his ears. Getting involved with a woman, especially a woman like Jasmine, hadn't been in his plans. He'd come back to Whitehorn for one reason. And one reason alone.

To see that justice was done.

A justice that was thirty years past due.

The thought chilled him, cooling the heat of passion that raced like a fire through his veins. His brother had been murdered. He'd been brutally killed and his body dumped in an abandoned field. That was what had brought him back to Whitehorn.

Not the lure of a beautiful woman.

The fact that Jasmine was a member of the Kincaid family only complicated matters more. What he hadn't been able to tell her on the way back into town was that he'd had another feeling while at the Kincaid ranch house. As soon as he'd walked through the doors of the study, he'd been overcome by the lingering presence of his brother's soul. Storm had no doubt. He knew the study had been the last place his brother had been alive.

Which told him only one thing. A Kincaid had been involved in his brother's murder.

A member of Jasmine's own family.

Storm sucked in a steadying breath and inhaled the delicate scent of wildflowers, Jasmine's scent. He moaned in frustration. Even with Jasmine miles away, his clothes still held the fragrant traces of their embrace. Steeling himself against the memory, he pressed his mouth in a resolute line and tasted the lingering sweetness of her lips.

He couldn't stop thinking about her. Or wanting her.

But he had no choice.

Later, when he had time to sort through his feelings, he would decide what to do about Jasmine. For now there was something else that needed his attention.

He had a long overdue visit to pay.

Nine

With no streetlights to guide him, the rough road leading into the Laughing Horse Reservation demanded all of his attention. The headlights of his car barely penetrated the thick darkness, making the potholes nearly impossible to see. Storm bounced over the ruts, wondering if the rented car's shock absorbers would hold out over the rugged terrain.

His white-knuckled grip tightened around the leather-wrapped steering wheel as he fought to ease the tension that filled him. He'd thought coming back to the reservation would be easier the second time around. But he'd been wrong. The painful memories of his past were just as sharp now as they had been earlier this afternoon.

Even more so, now that Jasmine wasn't beside him to ease the blow.

Being back on the reservation today and seeing the dilapidated house that had been his home, he'd been taken by surprise, rocked by the memories and shaken by unexpected emotions. And Jasmine...

Storm released a long, shaky breath. Jasmine had stood by him, waiting patiently for him to regain his control. Unlike most Anglos that he'd dealt with, she hadn't demanded answers, demanded to know everything he was feeling. Instead she'd listened quietly, letting him be the judge of how much he'd wanted to reveal.

And reveal he had.

He'd spilled out his entire miserable childhood to her. Storm's jaw clenched; his face warmed at the memory. Since leaving Whitehorn, he hadn't spoken of his past to anyone else. Even now he didn't understand why he'd felt the need to share it with Jasmine.

Or did he?

In the darkness the outline of the Tribal Center loomed up ahead, giving him an excuse to push his troubled thoughts aside. Storm slowed his car and eased into the parking lot. Turning off the ignition, he stared at the sprawling building. The huge complex housed the reservation's tribal offices, including those of the tribal leader, Jackson Hawk.

Storm had known Jackson since childhood. Once they'd been friends. Though they'd lost contact over the years, Jackson had been the one to track him down in New Mexico to tell him of the discovery of Raven's remains. Since his arrival in Whitehorn, however, Storm had only brief and impersonal contact with Jackson. His choice, not Jackson's, he admitted, shifting uneasily in his seat. Until now they'd met on neutral ground, never on reservation land. Storm had carefully insulated himself from his past the best he could.

But that was about to change.

Gathering his wavering resolve, he opened the door of the car and stepped out into the night. The air felt cool, bracing. The reservation seemed inordinately quiet, as though the community had drawn a hushed breath at his arrival. Climbing the stairs of the building, he paused to read the black letters painted on the door of the complex. Welcome To The Laughing Horse Tribal Center. Home Of The Northern Cheyenne Western Band.

Home. The cold palm of loneliness pressed its icy fingers against his back, chilling him. Laughing Horse had stopped being his home almost thirty years ago. Since then he'd lived and worked in New Mexico. But there he had no house, only an apartment. No family, since his job was his life. He had made no roots in the community to make it feel as though he truly belonged.

For the first time he realized he had no place to call his home.

Shaking off the bleak thought, Storm yanked open the door and stepped into the dimly lit building. A single light coming from an office down the hall marked his destination. His footsteps sounded too loud in the quiet building, making him feel as though he were an intruder. The weight of uncertainty pressed against his shoulders, slowing his step. Second thoughts eroded his confidence. His decision to come had been impulsive.

Perhaps he'd made a mistake.

Stopping just outside the doorway of the office, he peered inside. Jackson Hawk sat with his back to him, his long legs outstretched, his boot-clad feet propped on the sill of the window that overlooked the reservation grounds. He wore faded jeans and a white T-shirt. Hardly appropriate attire for a tribal official. But as Storm recalled from their youth, Jackson had always been something of a rebel.

Jackson's long black hair was pulled back into braids. From the reflection in the night-darkened window, Storm saw that his eyes were closed, the sharp features of his face relaxed. He hesitated in the doorway, debating whether or not to disturb the new tribal leader.

With his eyes still closed, Jackson murmured, "Well, Storm, my friend, are you staying or not?"

Storm flinched, the unexpectedness of the words startling him.

Smiling, Jackson opened his eyes. His feet hit the floor with a thud as he swiveled around to face him. "Don't look so surprised. I haven't turned psychic on you. Not yet, anyway." His grin deepening, he motioned to the window. "I happened to be watching when you pulled that fancy car of yours into the lot."

Fancy car. From anyone else it would have been considered just a casual remark. Coming from a fellow Cheyenne, it was a jab at his show of wealth, of his apparent adoption of the white man's ways. Storm stared at Jackson, his defenses on instant alert.

After a long moment Jackson filled the gaping silence. "I'm glad you're here, Storm. I wondered when you would finally come back to the reservation."

At the subtle censure in Jackson's tone, Storm's wariness grew. It took all of his willpower to not turn on his heel and run, to escape from this unsettling meeting. Instead, gathering his courage, he set his jaw in a determined line and said, "I'm here...for now."

Jackson rose to his feet, stretching to his full six-foot-plus height. Rounding the desk, he closed the distance between them. The two men stood eye-to-eye, their gazes guarded.

"So you're a big-shot lawyer in New Mexico," Jackson said, the words sounding like a taunt.

Anger flared inside Storm. Refusing to be baited into an argument, he returned calmly, "I have a practice in Albuquerque."

"A lucrative practice from what I can see." The man who'd once been his friend, raked an assessing glance, taking in his professionally styled haircut, the gold watch on his wrist and his casual yet expensive clothes. The corner of Jackson's mouth lifted into a smirk. "You've learned to blend in well with the white man's world."

"I didn't come to discuss my business practices,"

Storm said, unable to keep the defensive note from his voice.

Crossing his arms against his chest, Jackson sat on the edge of his desk. "Then why did you come?"

"I saw you this afternoon," Storm said.

"Ah, yes." Jackson nodded, his gaze thoughtful. "I wasn't sure if you'd noticed my presence. You were otherwise—" He tapped a finger against his chin, lifting a suggestive brow. "How shall I say it? You were occupied with a beautiful woman. A beautiful *white* woman."

Storm's hands balled into fists of rage at the innuendo. It took all of his strength to hold them stiffly at his sides. "You have no right to judge whom I choose to see."

"Someone has to use good judgment. It's obvious that you're not."

"What are you talking about?" The harsh demand reverberated throughout the small room. The force of the words surprised even himself. Coming here, Storm's intention had been to tell Jackson that he'd misread what he'd seen that afternoon. That there was nothing between him and Jasmine.

Instead he was defending his right to be with her.

Jackson's measuring gaze never wavered. "I'm talking about your involvement with a white woman. A Kincaid, no less."

The sharp reminder struck like a blow, leaving its mark.

"Did you forget? Raven died because he fell in love with a Kincaid," Jackson said, shaking his head and looking disappointed. "Can't you see that you're repeating your brother's mistake? You and I both know you're asking for more trouble than you can handle."

"Stay out of it, Jackson. It's none of your damn business," Storm said, his voice shaking with barely controlled emotion.

"Or what? Are you going to push me away, too, just like you pushed your family away when Raven died? Or have you lived so long in the white man's world that you don't even know when you're turning your back on your people?"

Hot anger flowed through him, setting his blood on fire. Storm's heart pounded in his chest, the sound echoing in his ears. "You don't know what you're talking about, Jackson. My parents pushed me out of their lives long before I left the reservation. They chose to drown themselves in alcohol. I wasn't going to stay and watch them do it. And I haven't forgotten my people. I've done more work for Native Americans than any other attorney—"

"In New Mexico perhaps. But not here in White-horn." Jackson stood, a vein pulsing at his temple, his face set in a hard, condemning line. "Why don't you admit it, Storm? You've shunned your life on Laughing Horse and the Cheyenne people. You've even found a white woman, a trophy wife to prove yourself worthy to live in the white man's world.''

In a blaze of red heat, something exploded deep inside him. Grabbing a fistful of Jackson's shirt, Storm slammed him against the wall. The impact shook the framed documents hanging nearby. Through clenched teeth, Storm said, ''Don't you ever talk about Jasmine in that way. She would never be any man's trophy wife. She's too special to settle for something like that.''

To his surprise, instead of continuing the argument, Jackson smiled.

At first Storm didn't understand the other man's reaction. Then, suddenly, the meaning became all too clear. His heart skipped a beat. His head felt light, as though he were floating above his body, as an observer, not a participant in this farce. He realized that he'd just been coerced into revealing his true feelings for Jasmine.

Slowly he released his old friend. His strength seemed to have seeped away with his anger. Raking his fingers through his hair, Storm sank into a nearby chair.

''I'm sorry, my friend. I never meant to hurt you,'' Jackson murmured, straightening his shirt as he returned to his seat on the edge of the desk. ''But I knew you would never admit to me, or to anyone, just how far your relationship with Jasmine had gone, if I didn't use a little deception. I had to know the truth.''

Storm shook his head. ''You want to know the truth? The truth is, I don't know what's happening between me and Jasmine.''

''But there is something,'' Jackson said.

Storm fell into an uneasy silence, unable to admit his own feelings, even to himself.

Jackson heaved a strained sigh. ''Storm, do you have any idea what you're getting yourself into—''

''I don't need a lecture, Jackson,'' Storm said, abruptly cutting him off. ''I know all the reasons why I should stay away from her.''

''Yet, you still see her.''

A statement, not a question. Storm felt the unnecessary need to explain. ''Jasmine's helping me. We're trying to find out the truth behind Raven's death.''

Jackson gave a harsh laugh. ''And you trust her? What if she discovers something that will hurt her family? Do you really think she'd betray them in order to help you?''

Struggling to hide his own uncertainty, Storm said, ''Jasmine is the most honest woman I have ever met, white or Native American. If she finds something that will answer the questions behind Raven's death, then she will tell me.''

Jackson didn't answer. The skeptical look in his eye spoke volumes.

He was wasting his time. Jackson was almost militant in his jaded opinion of the white man's intentions. Storm would never be able to change his mind. Feeling tired and defeated, more lost and alone than he'd ever felt before, he rose to his feet, unwilling to continue the useless debate.

Storm had returned to Whitehorn with the intention of finding peace, for himself and Raven. So far, all that he had found was bitterness and turmoil.

Without another word, he turned on his heel and headed for the door.

Before he'd gotten far, Jackson said, "It's not too late to come home, Storm. You can still be a part of our people's lives. Here on Laughing Horse you can make a difference."

Storm's step faltered. Reluctantly he turned to face his old friend.

"I know that I've told you this before, but now that I've taken over the duties of tribal chief, the council could use a new tribal lawyer." Jackson smiled, his sharp features softening with amusement. "Especially a lawyer who has had experience handling pro bono civil liberty cases."

His own words came to haunt him. Having no answer for his friend, Storm turned and left.

Her mother was waiting for her when she returned to the Big Sky Bed & Breakfast. She was outside on the porch, curled up on a wicker chair, sitting alone in the dark. Her quiet voice startled Jasmine as she climbed the front steps. "You're home, Jasmine."

"Mother, I didn't see you," Jasmine said, pressing a hand to her breast, stilling her pounding heart. She glanced through the closed doors into the brightly lit living room. "Where are our guests? And Aunt Yvette? Is anyone else here?"

"The Humphreys went into town for dinner. The Sterlings are taking a walk around the lake before they leave, also. Things have quieted down, so Yvette went home to be with your uncle Edward." Her mother motioned with a beringed hand to a nearby chair. "Sit down and join me."

Jasmine felt a shiver of trepidation at her mother's wooden tone. She knew her mother too well not to know that something was wrong. Reluctantly she did as her mother requested. She took a seat in the wicker rocking chair, sinking into the overstuffed cushion.

Despite the cool night air, Celeste wore only a thin cotton shirt and matching skirt, with no sweater or shawl. Her legs were bare, as were her feet. Her russet hair was unkempt, as though she'd dragged nervous fingers through its carefully coiffed style. The circles beneath her eyes looked even darker in the twilight hour, giving her a haunted expression.

Troubled by her mother's appearance, Jasmine reached out, covering her mother's trembling hand with her own. "What is it, Mother? What's wrong?"

"I've just gotten off the phone with Doris Atkins," Celeste said.

Jasmine's heart sank. Doris Atkins was the owner/manager of the hotel where Storm was staying. She was also a gossip. Mentally, Jasmine prepared herself for what was coming next.

Celeste's disappointed sigh whispered in the quiet night. "Are you going to tell me what you did today? And with whom? Or am I going to have to get my information secondhand from my supposed 'friends' in town?"

"Mother, I'm sorry." Jasmine tightened her hold on her mother's hand. "I should have been honest with you."

"Yes, you should have." Celeste clung to her, her grip desperate. "You were with Storm Hunter today, weren't you?"

Her voice barely a whisper, Jasmine said, "Yes, Mother. I was."

Celeste loosened her grip, then pulled her hand away. Crossing her arms at her waist, she held herself tight, as though she'd been physically wounded by the admission. "Can't you see what you're doing? This relationship with Storm is doomed from the start." She shook her head, looking older than her years. "We may not be the Capulets and the Montagues, but there is bad blood between the Kincaids and the Hunters. Jasmine, I don't want to see you hurt."

Unwanted tears filled Jasmine's eyes, blurring her vision. The rift between her and her mother was growing, and she felt powerless to stop it. Swallowing hard at the lump of emotion that had stuck in her throat, she said, "I know all the reasons why I should stay away from Storm. But I can't, Mother. There's something between us, something I can't ignore. I'm falling in love with him."

Celeste closed her eyes and leaned forward in her chair, giving a low, mewling sound of pain.

Jasmine started to reach out to her, to comfort her, but she stopped, not sure that she could give her mother the solace she needed. Instead she said, "Mother, I don't know what's going to happen between me and Storm. But you've always encouraged me to follow my instincts. Well, my instinct is to listen to my heart. And my heart is telling me I have to see where these feelings for Storm will take me."

Slowly, Celeste straightened. Though pale and shaky, she rose to her feet.

Jasmine stood, facing her mother.

Gathering her daughter into her arms, Celeste held her tightly. "I love you, Jasmine," she whispered, "I just hope you won't be hurt by your decision."

With that, Celeste released her. She whirled and hurried to the front door. Her bare feet padding softly against the wooden floor, she disappeared into the house, leaving Jasmine to stand alone on the front porch.

Her body shaking from the impact of what had just occurred, Jasmine sat down hard, collapsing back into the wicker chair. The night felt colder, darker. She pulled her knees up, tucking them under her chin, hugging her legs with her arms. Around her she heard the sounds of the Montana wildlife, the cracking of a twig underfoot, the quiet scurry of an animal's step and the distant flap of a bird's wing. Around her, the rich scent of the pine trees filled the air.

She took comfort most nights from the rustic charm of her surroundings. Tonight she felt only solitude and loneliness.

Her mother's parting words echoed over and over again in her mind. *I just hope you won't be hurt by your decision.*

Jasmine's dismal mood sank a notch lower as she realized it was as much of a sign of approval as she could hope of getting from her mother.

Jasmine slept fitfully. The wee hours of the night passed slowly as she listened to her mother's restless pacing in the room down the hall. Though she wanted to go to Celeste, to try to ease her concerns, she knew she couldn't allow herself to do it.

For she knew in her heart she was the cause of her mother's pain and distress.

Finally Jasmine closed her eyes and succumbed to an exhausted sleep. But not for long. Just before dawn, she felt a hand on her shoulder, shaking her. Someone calling her name.

"Jasmine?" It was her mother's voice. Yet it sounded so strange, so flat and emotionless. Jasmine blinked, wincing as the sandy grit of sleeplessness burned her eyes. "Wake up, Jasmine. I need you."

Alarmed, Jasmine sat up. "Mother? What's wrong?"

The table lamp was switched on and she shielded her eyes against the sudden brightness. It took a moment before she could focus on Celeste standing beside her bed, wrapped in a terry-cloth bathrobe. In the dim light, her mother's face was so pale against her russet hair that she looked like a ghost.

Despite her distraught appearance, Celeste's voice remained unnaturally calm. "I can't tell you. Not now, Jasmine. I've called the family. They'll be here soon. As soon as you're ready, come downstairs. I'll explain everything then."

With that ominous bit of information, she turned from the bed and left the room.

Jasmine's heart seemed to have stopped beating. For a long moment she sat frozen in her bed, unable to move. She stared at the empty doorway through which her mother had disappeared, forgetting to breathe. These past few months she'd sensed her mother was deeply troubled, that she was teetering on the edge of some sort of spiritual reckoning.

It would seem the time had finally come.

Her lungs burning in her chest, Jasmine gulped in a cooling draft of air. Her hands trembled as she pushed aside the bedcovers. Swinging her feet to the floor, she stood on unsteady legs.

Forcing herself to move, she hurried to the dresser and pulled out a pair of jeans. She slipped them on beneath her nightshirt. Tying the long ends of her oversize T-shirt at her waist, she left her feet bare and hurried from the room.

Hushed voices sounded from the kitchen as she made her way down the back staircase. Her mouth watered at the welcoming scent of coffee. She would need more than one cupful of the fortifying liquid to wake her groggy senses.

Aunt Yvette and Uncle Edward were seated at the kitchen table. Yvette, with her gray hair and striking features, looked worried. Edward had a hand on his wife's shoulder, absently rubbing it in soothing circles. They glanced up at her when she entered the room. From the troubled expressions on their faces, it was apparent they hadn't a clue what this family meeting was all about.

Before she could greet them, the back door banged open. Bringing with her a draft of cold morning air, her sister, Cleo, entered the kitchen. "I got here as soon as I could," she said in a breathless tone. Her thick russet hair was uncombed and tangled. She wore a beige trench coat over her pajama pants, looking as though she'd just jumped out of bed. "Summer's parking her car. She'll be here in just a minute."

The door opened again. Summer breezed in, bringing David, Yvette and Edward's son, along with her. Her eyes widened in alarm as she glanced around the room, taking in the gathering of familiar faces. A deep frown creased her brow. "I came as soon as I could. Gavin is at home with Alyssa. What's happened? Where's Celeste?"

A cacophony of voices erupted at once, each talking, but no one seeming to know what had brought them together. The one person with all the answers to their questions was nowhere in sight. Worriedly Jasmine paced the room. This couldn't go on, she had to find her mother.

As though she'd read her mind, Celeste entered the kitchen. A hush fell across the room. All eyes were riveted upon the frazzled features of her normally lovely face.

Jasmine's chest tightened with apprehension, making it difficult to breathe.

Still dressed in her terry-cloth robe, Celeste looked numbly from one person to the other. Frowning slightly, she said, "Where's Frannie?"

"With Austin," Yvette said, wringing her hands together in a helpless gesture. "Remember, Celeste? I told you there was a NASCAR event this weekend. She travels with him whenever he's out of town."

"Of course, I forgot," Celeste said, looking chagrined. She sighed, giving a satisfied nod. "Everyone else is here."

"What's this all about, Celeste?" Yvette asked, rising to her feet.

"No, sit down please. Everyone." Celeste motioned to the table, waiting for them to take their seats.

Exchanging nervous glances, Summer and Cleo took a seat at the table. Jasmine remained standing, as did David. He stood next to her at the kitchen counter, an unreadable expression on his lean face.

Celeste seemed oddly calm in the wake of their rising unease. Her voice sounded hollow, almost void of emotion, when she asked, "Would anyone like a cup of coffee before we begin?"

"Celeste," Summer said, her voice filled with uncharacteristic impatience, "this isn't a tea party. You called us here for a reason. I for one am anxious to know that reason."

"Yes, Mother," Cleo said, unbuckling her trench coat and revealing a yellow print pajama top. "What's going on? What couldn't wait until morning for us to hear?"

With shaking hands, Celeste reached into the pocket of her terry-cloth robe and withdrew a gun. Taking a deep breath, she placed it in the center of the table.

Though she knew little about guns, Jasmine saw

the markings identifying it as a Colt .45. She felt her heart thud against her chest.

Beside her, David stiffened. He took a step toward the table, then stopped. Standing uneasily, a deep frown of concern furrowed his brow.

Cleo and Summer looked helplessly at each other, confusion obvious in their eyes.

Yvette shrank back in her chair. Edward's arm went around her in a gesture of support. Encouraged, Yvette was the first to speak. "What's this all about, Celeste? This was Jeremiah's gun. What are you doing with it?"

"I've had it for years, thirty years to be exact. I've kept it so well hidden I nearly forgot about it myself." Celeste swayed unsteadily on her feet. Grasping the back of a nearby chair, she closed her eyes, as though trying to gather her strength. Then, opening them, she slowly glanced at each of them, her gaze regretful.

"I've asked each of you to come here to tell you…"

Her voice trembled and broke with emotion. With a sigh she cast her eyes downward. Then, the words so soft they had to strain to hear her, she said, "It was me…. I killed him. I killed Raven Hunter."

Ten

Jasmine stood motionless, feeling as though the bottom had just dropped out of her world. She couldn't believe her own ears. Her kind and gentle mother, a woman who'd lived her life in the pursuit of spiritual peace and harmony, had just confessed to a murder.

It wasn't possible.

The whole idea was absurd.

Despite her own denials, Jasmine's vision blurred as a picture of Storm's pain-lined face cropped up in her mind. She closed her eyes against the sting of tears, unable to bear the image. Her mother's uncharacteristic objections to her seeing Storm echoed in her mind. No wonder Celeste didn't want her to be with him. She'd been afraid of what might be revealed. All this time Jasmine had been helping Storm look for the murderer of his brother and the truth was right in front of her, in the fold of her own family.

No! With a jerk, Jasmine opened her eyes. She forced herself to look at her mother, to see her as she really was, frightened and more fragile than ever before. She shook her head. No, it couldn't be true. Her mother wouldn't have deceived her all this time. She wouldn't have lied to her own daughter.

"Celeste," David said, the first to break the spell of silence that had held the room. His gentle voice jarred Jasmine from her trance of disbelief. "Raven Hunter has been dead for thirty years. If you killed him, why haven't you told anyone before now?"

Celeste looked at him, a plea for understanding in her tired expression. "Because I didn't know for sure."

"But you're sure now," David said, keeping his voice even, with no hint of censure.

"Tonight I had another dream," Celeste said, her voice distant and hollow. She stared straight ahead at a spot on the kitchen wall, her eyes glazed and unfocused. It was as though she were reliving a memory, and not truly aware of what was happening here and now.

"A dream," David coaxed, gently prodding her to continue. "What sort of dream?"

"A dream that isn't really a dream." Blinking away the stupor, Celeste sighed. Wearily she took a seat at the kitchen table. Unable to face them, she studied her hands that she held tightly clasped in her lap. "It was a vision from the past. A memory that I've spent thirty years trying to forget. But now I know the truth. I finally know what happened on the night Raven Hunter died."

Yvette scooted her chair next to Celeste's. Wrapping an arm around her sister's shoulder, she said, "We all love you, Celeste. No matter what, you know that we'll always support you. Please don't be afraid to tell us what happened."

Murmurs of agreement sounded throughout the room.

Still too stunned to speak, Jasmine remained unforgivably silent.

With her eyes still downcast, Celeste began to speak, spilling out the guilty memory that had haunted her dreams for almost thirty years. "It all started when Jeremiah discovered Blanche's pregnancy. When she admitted that Raven Hunter was the father, Jeremiah nearly went insane. I—I'd never seen him so angry before. He looked wild, and filled with hatred. I thought for sure he'd do something to Raven…to hurt him in some way."

Celeste stopped and shuddered at the thought.

Yvette squeezed her shoulder, silently giving her encouragement.

Celeste covered her sister's hand with hers, clinging to it, then continued, "Instead of lashing out at him, Jeremiah paid Raven to leave town. No one expected Raven to accept the money. But when he did, Jeremiah made sure everyone knew, including Blanche. It nearly killed Blanche to hear the news. Something died in her after that. The disappointment she must have felt—"

Her voice broke. Tears filled her eyes. Celeste

blinked rapidly, allowing a single drop to cascade down her pale cheek. The words thick with emotion, she said, "I never believed Raven would leave Blanche. I knew he would change his mind. It shouldn't have been a surprise that he'd come back to the ranch."

Celeste looked directly at Summer, her gaze fierce and determined. "Raven was a good man. He wouldn't have abandoned Blanche or you, Summer. I'm sure the reason he returned was to give Jeremiah back the money."

Summer nodded her understanding, her smile hesitant.

Celeste looked at the gun she'd placed on the kitchen table. Her gaze terrified, she said, "I was in bed, trying to sleep. But there was a terrible thunderstorm that night and I couldn't relax. That was when I heard the shouts, the angry voices coming from the study. I didn't know who was downstairs, or what was happening. I recognized Jeremiah's voice, but no one else's. I was frightened and not sure what to do. I knew Jeremiah kept a gun in his dresser drawer. So I went to his room and got out the Colt.

"When I went downstairs, I only saw the back of a man's head. He'd pinned Jeremiah to the floor, and he was beating him with his fists."

Celeste choked back a sob. She lifted a hand to her mouth and closed her eyes, struggling for control.

Yvette and Summer both looked close to tears.

Cleo looked shocked, devastated by the events unfolding in front of her. David and Edward wore looks of resignation and utter sympathy.

Pain knifed Jasmine's heart as she shared her mother's distress. She wanted to go to her, to comfort her, to stop this tragic testimony. But something held her back. She needed to know the truth, once and for all.

Regaining her composure, Celeste opened her eyes. "I couldn't see the man's face. I only heard an angry voice shouting…'if you get in our way again, I'll kill you, old man.' I—I was so afraid that whoever was attacking Jeremiah meant those words. I tried to stop him. I called out, begging the man to let Jeremiah go. But he wouldn't listen. I don't think he even heard me. He was so intent on hurting Jeremiah, I knew I had no choice—"

Celeste lifted her trembling hands and stared at them. "My hands were shaking so badly, I don't know how I was able to hold the gun straight. But I knew I had to do something, before Jeremiah was killed. So I closed my eyes, and I pulled the trigger on the Colt." Tears poured down her face. "At the same time, th-there was a clap of thunder outside. It shook the house, and scared me so. I thought it was God's way of condemning me. Then I smelled smoke, coming from the gun in my hand…it was so strong and bitter, it made me sick to my stomach. I opened my eyes and dropped the Colt on the floor, appalled by what I'd done. That was when the intruder slumped to the floor and I finally saw his face. Jeremiah was safe, but I had killed Raven Hunter.''

Summer looked away, seeming unwilling to let Celeste see the tears filling her eyes. Though Jasmine's own eyes remained dry, they burned with unshed emotion.

''Somehow, Jeremiah got to his feet. He told me to stay put while he examined Raven's body,'' Celeste said. She shook her head, giving a quick bitter-sounding laugh. ''I was so shocked by what had just happened, I couldn't have moved even if I'd wanted to. When Jeremiah told me Raven was dead, I lost what little control I had and became hysterical. I never meant for anything like that to happen. Jeremiah tried to calm me, he told me he'd take care of everything. He said it would be our little secret, that no one would ever find out that I'd killed Raven.''

Her shoulders slumped as she heaved a defeated sigh. ''I never knew what he'd done with the body. I did know what I had done was wrong, but I tried to push the memory of that night from my mind. Over time, I succeeded. It wasn't until Raven's remains were found that I began to remember that night.''

''That was why you could never say no to Jeremiah,'' Yvette said softly, shaking her head. ''Why you never could stand up to him when he tried to control your life.''

''He held all the cards,'' Celeste admitted. ''He

knew the worst secret in the world. If I didn't do what he wanted, I knew he could ruin me. That was why, when Ty Monroe came to town and asked me to marry him, I agreed. The thought of moving as far away as Baton Rouge was like a dream come true. At that point, I'd have done anything to get away from Jeremiah.''

Celeste looked anxiously at each of her daughters. ''Don't misunderstand me. In my own way I loved your father. He was a good man. Being with him saved my sanity.''

At last Jasmine's tears found release. Teardrops fell unchecked down her cheeks. The last of the puzzle had fallen into place. She now understood her mother's fascination with the spiritual hereafter, her frantic pursuit of peace and solace. All these years she'd repressed a traumatic event. But the tragedy had never completely disappeared. What had occurred in the study that night had haunted Celeste's dreams and her subconscious every day of her life. It wasn't any wonder that she'd sought alternate means to find absolution.

''What happens now?'' Yvette asked, looking to her son for an answer.

David made his way to Celeste's side. Crouching on a bent knee, he looked her in the eye and said, ''We'll need to make a report. The police will have to be notified.''

Celeste nodded. ''I know. That's what I want. I've

lived too many years with this secret. It's time to tell the truth."

"Then I'll go with you." David clasped her hands in his. "I'll be with you every step of the way."

"So will I," Yvette said, a determined look on her face. "You'll always have my support."

Edward nodded. Cleo and Summer murmured their own agreements. Everyone stood, voicing their opinions, making suggestions on the best way to handle the tenuous situation.

Jasmine remained motionless at the kitchen counter, unable to join her family, torn between her loyalty to her mother and her newfound feelings for Storm. She knew Storm would be shocked by the news. He would be angry and upset, and rightly so. How could she ever convince him that she hadn't intentionally kept the truth from him?

But if he didn't believe her, the fragile bond they'd built between them would be destroyed.

Jasmine felt overwhelmed by what might be lost. Before she'd met Storm, she'd dated many different men. But no one had ever caught her heart. No one she could say that's him, he's the one she'd spend her life with. She'd watched with an envious eye as others in her family had found happiness with their one true love. All the while, wondering when it would be her turn.

Then Storm had come crashing into her world and she knew something special was about to happen.

He'd given her life meaning, a new purpose. She finally understood what it meant to care about someone so deeply that nothing else in the world mattered but him.

For her, it was love at first sight. From the moment they'd first met, she'd had no doubt that they were meant to be together.

But fate seemed to be working against them.

Knowing she had no other choice, Jasmine pushed herself from the kitchen counter. Slowly she made her way to her mother's side. Sensing her presence, Celeste turned to face her. Jasmine saw the painful glimmer of remorse in her mother's eyes and the heart-wrenching plea for understanding.

No one but Celeste would know the effect her confession would have on Jasmine's life. Her voice trembling, she said, "I'm so sorry, Jasmine."

"I know, I know…" Jasmine folded her mother into an embrace. "It'll be all right, Mother," she whispered. "We'll work this out together. Everything will be fine."

Jasmine wished she believed the words to be true in her own heart.

Shortly after noon, Storm felt the first inkling of unease. Jasmine had told him that she had to work in the morning, that she couldn't see him until that afternoon. He took a steadying breath, struggling to get a hold on his impatience. It was still early, he told himself.

There was no need to start worrying yet.

When one o'clock came and went, he knew something was wrong. For the past thirty minutes he'd been pacing the floor, trying not to let his imagination run away from him. Jasmine should have called or stopped in by now. She was too honest and open. It wasn't like her not to let him know that her plans had changed.

Unless her family's objections had finally gotten to her. Unless she'd decided she couldn't see him again, after all.

The grim thought spurred him into action. He strode to the phone, picked up the receiver and started punching in the number for the B and B. The possibility of Celeste answering stopped him. The last thing he wanted was to make trouble for Jasmine. At least, no more than he'd already caused.

Frustrated, Storm slammed the receiver back onto its cradle. He pushed the hair from his face and smacked his palm flat against the wall. The sound reverberated throughout the quiet room. His hand smarted, doing little to help his foul mood. He'd been cooped up inside too long. He had to get out. He had to do something.

He needed to find Jasmine—even if it meant climbing the walls of the bed-and-breakfast to get to her.

Grabbing his keys, he headed for the door. Just as

he was about to open it, three sharp raps sounded on the other side.

Jasmine....

Relief poured through him, easing the tension from his muscles. He shook his head, feeling foolish for letting his insecurities get the better of him. With a sheepish smile, he opened the door.

And was greeted by the somber face of Gretchen Neal. Behind her stood a tall, brown-haired, blue-eyed man, dressed in the uniform of a deputy sheriff.

Storm's smile fled. He stared at them, his heart lurching in his chest. His first thoughts were of Jasmine, that something had happened to her. She'd been hurt, injured, and the police had come to tell him the bad news.

As soon as it surfaced, he discarded the unlikely thought. No one knew of his fledgling relationship with Jasmine. As far as the town of Whitehorn was concerned, he'd be the last person to be notified of a Kincaid's demise.

The police were here for a very different reason.

Which meant only one thing—Raven.

"What is it?" Storm demanded in lieu of a greeting.

Gretchen Neal winced at his gruff tone. Looking as though she were struggling to control her own impatience, she inhaled a steadying breath. With a nod toward the man behind her, she said, "Mr. Hunter, this is Deputy Reed Austin. If you have a moment, we'd like to talk to you.''

"About what?'' Storm said, not budging from the doorway, his hand still clenching the doorknob in a death grip.

"There's been a development in your brother's case." She glanced up and down the hotel walkway, as though checking for eavesdroppers. "Would you mind if we came inside and talked about it?''

Storm stepped back, letting them enter the room. A development... The words brought a quivering of trepidation to the pit of his belly, making him even more keenly aware of Jasmine's absence. He refused to consider the possibility that she could be connected to this new development in any way. All he knew for certain was that without her at his side, he felt exposed, vulnerable to whatever news Detective Neal was about to give him.

He wasn't sure if he could handle this on his own.

Refusing to give in to his fears, he said, "What sort of development?''

Gretchen nodded toward the room's only chair. "Would you like to sit down, Mr. Hunter?''

Storm crossed his arms against his chest and planted his feet firmly on the carpeted floor. He looked at her, challenging her to delay the news any further.

At his uncooperative response, Deputy Reed Austin shifted uncomfortably, one foot to the other, his gaze narrow, his stance wary. Obviously the man's presence was a result of the confrontation between Storm and David Hannon, which had occurred when he'd first arrived in town. Storm decided the deputy must be here in a show of support to his comrade, to make sure that no harm would come to Detective Neal from a "hotheaded Indian."

Choosing each word with care, Gretchen said, "There's been a break in the case. We're holding a suspect at the county jail."

"A suspect?" Storm frowned, unable to believe what he was hearing. All these years he'd thought Jeremiah Kincaid was the one who'd killed his brother. But Jeremiah was dead. Now this woman, this detective, was telling him that someone else committed the crime. He wasn't sure what to think.

"It's a solid lead," Gretchen said, her tone defensive, as though she'd read the doubts in his mind. "This person... They've confessed to the shooting."

Storm almost wished he'd listened to her advice and had chosen to sit, after all. His legs felt weak and wobbly. He wasn't sure if they were strong enough to hold him. His voice sounding hoarse with suppressed emotion, he said, "Who is it? Who killed my brother?"

Hesitating, Gretchen glanced at her partner. Deputy Austin nodded his encouragement. Turning back to Storm, she said stiffly, "Celeste Monroe came in early this morning. She's confessed to the crime."

Celeste Monroe.

Jasmine's mother.

The news struck like a blow, winding him. This time Storm did sit down. He collapsed into the wooden straight-backed chair, stunned by the revelation.

Gretchen continued, but the buzz of disbelief running through his head made her voice sound odd, as though she were speaking to him through a tunnel. "Mrs. Monroe is being held in the sheriff's custody, until her arraignment tomorrow morning. If you have any further questions, please feel free to call me, or Sheriff Rawlings, at the station."

Storm realized she was winding down her speech, preparing to leave. Riveting his gaze at her, he said, "There's got to be some mistake."

Gretchen looked at him, and the wooden expression she'd worn since stepping into his hotel room slipped from its place. He saw the uncertainty in her gaze and remembered that she, too, had a connection to the Kincaid family. The word around town was that she and David Hannon were engaged.

She shook her head. "It's a strong lead. Mrs. Monroe was able to give us a detailed account of the crime. Plus, she's turned over the murder weapon."

The last of Storm's doubts dissolved. Unable to stop himself, he recalled Celeste's initial reaction to his presence in Whitehorn. It must have been his resemblance to Raven that had brought the shocked look to her face before she'd collapsed into a dead faint. Time and again, Jasmine had professed her mother's normally liberated views. Now Celeste's objections to his seeing Jasmine made more sense. She had murdered his brother. It wasn't any wonder that she wanted to keep them apart.

"Mr. Hunter, are you listening to me?"

Storm blinked. Startled, he glanced up at the detective. He'd been so lost in his own thoughts he'd forgotten her presence.

Frowning, Gretchen said, "We're leaving now, Mr. Hunter. If there's anything more we can do..." She let the words fade.

"There's nothing more to be done. It's over." Storm shook his head, giving a mirthless laugh. "It's finally over."

Gretchen hesitated, studying him, her concern obvious.

Deputy Austin cleared his throat, motioning toward the door. Gretchen turned to leave. With her hand on the doorknob, she paused and said, "I'm sorry the investigation didn't go as quickly as you'd hoped. A lot of time has passed since your brother's death. There just weren't that many leads to follow."

Storm nodded, unable to answer. His frustration at the police department's lack of progress seemed minute compared to the crippling sense of betrayal that was growing inside him. Now he understood Jasmine's absence.

Without another word, Detective Neal and Deputy Austin left his hotel room, closing the door behind them.

For a long moment Storm remained in the chair, immobilized by shock and disbelief. He felt crushed, as though he'd been run over by a semitrailer. For thirty years, Celeste had kept her guilt a secret. He didn't understand how she could have lived with herself.

Was the killing of an Indian so unimportant that it didn't bother her?

The acrid taste of bitterness rose in his throat, making him feel sick to his stomach. The chasm he'd always felt between the whites and the Native Americans deepened. His heart thudded painfully against his chest. What hurt most, even more than Celeste's callous indifference, was Jasmine's betrayal.

As Jackson Hawk had predicted, Jasmine had kept the truth from him. How long had she known of her mother's guilty secret? Was her pledge to help him nothing more than a ruse? Just a way for her to throw him off track?

A surge of self-disgust propelled him to his feet. He paced the floor, giving vent to his growing anger. Like a sheep, he'd allowed her to lead him astray. Certainly his desire for her had been a potent distraction. Jasmine had used him and his own weaknesses to keep him from discovering the truth.

How could he have been so blind?

As he struggled with a growing bout of self-recrimination, a hesitant knock sounded at the door.

Storm froze, stopping midpace. He stared at the door. His first impulse was to ignore the knock, giving the unexpected visitor no choice but to leave. He was in no mood for more bad news.

But a higher force overrode his good judgment. Ignoring the voice of reason, he moved to the door. Deep in his heart, he knew who had come calling. He told himself that delaying the confrontation would only prolong the inevitable heartbreak.

It was time he faced what fate had brought him.

Bracing himself, he opened the door. And found Jasmine waiting for him.

Jasmine's breath caught painfully in her throat. From the look in Storm's eyes, she realized she was too late. He'd already heard the news. He knew the truth about her mother.

Nervously she licked her lips. "Storm—"

"Whatever you have to say, I'm not interested," he said, cutting her off, his voice hard and unforgiving. "I've heard enough lies to last me a lifetime."

"I didn't lie to you, Storm," she said, slowly shaking her head. "You have to believe me. I didn't know about any of this until this morning."

"This morning?" He glanced at his wristwatch. "It's almost two o'clock in the afternoon. It's certainly taken you long enough to find me to tell me the news.''

"Storm, please—"

The hotel's housekeeper walked by, pushing a cleaning cart, her gaze curious. The plump, dark-haired woman paused outside the room next door, busying herself with checking inventory. But more likely she was giving herself a chance to eavesdrop.

After the frustrating morning she'd spent at the sheriff's office waiting to hear the outcome of her mother's fate, the last thing Jasmine needed was to be further humiliated by being caught in a heated argument with Storm outside his hotel room. With all the pride she could muster, she lifted her chin and said, "If you don't mind, I'd prefer to discuss this in private. May I come in?"

Jasmine steeled herself for a rejection.

To her surprise, without arguing, Storm stepped back and allowed her to enter.

Jasmine's legs felt unsteady as she made her way into his hotel room, her strength gone. Memories of the first time she'd been here, of the steamy embrace they'd shared, crept into her mind. She brushed away the untimely image, knowing she needed her full wits about her to convince Storm of her innocence.

The door closed with a loud click, setting her nerves even further on edge. Slowly she turned to face him.

His steely gaze flitted over her before he pushed

past her to stand at the opposite side of the room, putting distance between them. Jasmine's heart sank further when he refused to look at her.

Not allowing herself to give up, she made her plea for understanding. "Storm, my mother never confided in me. Her confession... It's been just as much a shock to me as it must be to you. I didn't know about any of this until this morning. You have to believe me."

"I don't have to believe anything," he said, his icy tone sending a shiver down her spine. "I don't know why you bothered to come here. You're wasting your time, Jasmine. I want nothing more to do with you, or your family."

The sharp words cut her to the quick, leaving a raw and open wound in her heart. Despite the blow, she refused to admit defeat. She refused to believe that the bond they'd built, the precious moments they'd shared, had been for nothing.

If he thought she would give up so easily, he was wrong.

"That's it?" she demanded, letting the anger rise in her voice. "One thing goes wrong, and you're ready to toss aside everything that we've shared?"

"It's more than just one thing," he said, biting out the words. "Your mother killed my brother."

"But I didn't know—" Her voice broke. Tears of frustration blurred her vision. She blinked hard, refusing to allow anything to stop her. "I've never lied to you, Storm. You have to know that's true."

He remained stubbornly mute. Standing with his hands on his hips, his face set in a harsh line, he wouldn't meet her gaze.

Jasmine shook her head, letting the tears of frustration fill her eyes. Her voice trembling with emotion, she said, "You can't let yourself believe me, can you? If you do, then you'd have to let go of all that hate and resentment you've built up all these years toward my family. You said you'd come back to Whitehorn to see justice done for your brother. But that isn't true. This isn't really about Raven, is it?"

A vein pulsed at his temple. His jaw clenched and unclenched. But he refused to answer.

"This was never just about Raven," she said, forcing herself to continue. "Raven's just an excuse you've used to push everyone out of your life. I know you were hurt deeply. But you've used your past as a reason never to let yourself get close to anyone else."

Still, he wouldn't answer.

Despite the helpless frustration rising inside her, Jasmine knew she had to finish what she'd started. "Raven wasn't the only one who died all those years ago. A part of you died, also. The part that's capable of caring about others. Can't you see? You've got your feelings so bottled up inside, you can't allow yourself to love someone enough to forgive even the worst of mistakes.''

Storm's silence spoke volumes. He turned his head and looked away, not saying a word.

Feeling the sting of his rejection, Jasmine took a quick, steadying breath. She had tried to get through to him and had failed. There was nothing more for her to do.

Gathering her shattered pride, she wiped the tears from her face and said, ''I want you to know something, Storm. No matter what's happened here today, I won't forget the time that we spent together...or what could have been between us. I will always care about you.''

With her heart feeling as though it had split in two, she turned to leave.

Eleven

"Jasmine, wait."

The words escaped his mouth before he had a chance to think them through. It wasn't like Storm to act on impulse, to let his heart rule his actions, but right now his heart wouldn't let her walk out that door.

To his relief, Jasmine stopped. Slowly she turned to face him.

For the first time he really looked at her. The red, cap-sleeved T-shirt was coming untucked from the waistband of her black slacks. Her dark hair looked mussed, as though she hadn't taken the time to comb it into place. Her makeup was nonexistent, emphasizing the paleness of her complexion, the weariness etching her face and the dark circles beneath her eyes. And he knew she hadn't told him the complete truth.

She, too, was suffering.

Her mother had kept a devastating secret from her and her family. A secret that had destroyed the balance of their lives, as it had his. Jasmine, of all people, understood the pain and disillusionment that he felt.

But she understood more than just his pain. She knew of his weaknesses, as well. What she'd said, it was as though she had looked into his very soul and had seen his worst fears.

She knew why he had never allowed himself to get close to anyone else. The only person he'd ever truly cared about had been Raven. When Raven disappeared, he'd felt his loss as a rejection. That was the real reason he'd run away from his life on Laughing Horse. Because he couldn't allow himself to acknowledge just how much his brother's "abandonment" had hurt.

She was right about his resentment toward her family, too. When Raven left, instead of letting himself accept the worst, that his brother simply didn't care about him, Storm had blamed the Kincaids for his disappearance. Being proven correct seemed little compensation for the years he'd wasted, allowing his resentment to fester into a crippling distrust of all whites.

And now Jasmine stood in front of him, the same woman he'd waited so anxiously to see only minutes before. The same beautiful woman who had the power to set his blood on fire with a single look.

The same woman with whom he'd allowed himself to fall in love.

Silence echoed in the room. Fear tightened his chest, making it hard to draw a breath. Even now, he couldn't put into words what he felt in his heart. He couldn't run the risk of another abandonment.

He would rather be safe and live his life alone.

But that didn't stop him from wanting her, from needing to feel the reassuring warmth of her body next to his. Unable to stop himself, he crossed the room and closed the distance between them. For just a moment he studied her, memorizing the sculpted lines of her exotic face, the gut-wrenching tears that she tried so hard to hide, and the stubborn yet fragile pride in the tilt of her head.

Storm bit back an oath, his anger directed at himself. She'd come asking for understanding. Instead of listening, he'd pushed her away. His behavior had been inexcusable. He didn't deserve her forgiveness. He didn't deserve a second chance. Still he longed for the sweet redemption he could find only in her arms.

His voice thick with emotion, he whispered, "Jasmine, I'm sorry."

Something seemed to melt inside her. The tension gripping her body loosened its hold. Fresh tears welled in her eyes as a sob of relief escaped from her lips. With a shake of her head, she said, "Oh, Storm."

He wasn't sure who reached out first. But it didn't really matter. Somehow they found themselves wrapped in each other's arms, clinging to each other for support.

Relief poured through him as he held her close, savoring the feel of her slender body next to his. He buried his hand in the short strands of her dark hair, cradling the back of her head. He tipped her face upward to his, forcing her to look at him. With the pad of his thumb, he wiped the trail of tears from her cheek, then showered the spot with soft, delicate kisses. His lips grazed her temple, the hollow of her cheek, the tip of her chin, before settling on her irresistible mouth.

Beneath his gentle assault, she closed her eyes and inhaled a shaky draft of air. Her quiet exhalation sounded in his ears, her breath fanning his skin.

He lowered his hands to measure the narrow width of her waist. His fingers skimmed her breasts, stroking the turgid centers. Her body quickened, tensing beneath his touch. Through the thin fabric of her shirt, he felt her nipples contract and harden.

His own body responded in kind. A warm rush of heat flooded his groin. He moaned, as Jasmine shifted her stance, brushing her tummy against his arousal. Never before had he felt such sweet misery.

He took her mouth in a greedy kiss, plunging his tongue into her moist heat, finding his own taste of heaven. She gave as much as she took, opening her mouth to his, staking her own claim.

The last of his self-control evaporated in a blaze of red heat. With his arms still firmly around her, he backstepped toward the bed, half carrying, half leading her every step of the way. The edge of the mattress caught the backs of his knees. He fell, sprawling spread-eagle against the soft bedcovers.

Jasmine landed on top of him, one leg wedged between his thighs, her body straddling his. The box-spring sighed in protest at the unexpectedness of their combined weight. She dug her elbows into his chest and lifted herself to look at him. Her gaze was so wide-eyed and innocent that for a moment second thoughts caught up to him. His mind raced with all the reasons he should put a stop to this, before they went any further.

Then a slow, tentative smile touched her face. Slowly, deliberately, she lowered her head and kissed him. Just a fleeting touch of her lips against his. A kiss meant to tease, to test his willingness. She nibbled on his lower lip, tugging it through her teeth. Her tongue lashed against his mouth, making him close his eyes against a growing desire.

Following the chiseled line of his jaw, she dropped butterfly kisses onto the smooth skin of his face. Pushing his long hair out of her way, she nuzzled his neck and bit down onto the lobe of his ear, giving it a gentle tug.

Storm let her have her way, until he could stand no more. With a growl of impatience, he anchored his hands around her waist and rolled her onto her back. She fell against the tousled bedcovers, staring up at him, with a look that only fueled his desire. She was an irresistible combination of innocence and seduction.

Tacitly they acknowledged that both of them were wearing too much clothing. Storm pulled the ends of her shirt out of her waistband, lifting it over her head. The black lacy brassiere gave him pause. Recovering his composure, with a quick, deft movement, he unhooked the center clasp, exposing her beautiful body for him to see.

With an impatience of her own, Jasmine struggled with the buttons of his shirt. Her fingers fumbled over the openings, wasting much too much precious time. Obligingly he tore the shirt open, the buttons popping their threads in protest. Tossing the ruined shirt aside, he focused his attention on more important matters. Gently he circled the tips of his fingers around one rounded breast, then the other, noting the contrast of his dark, coppery skin against her pale, creamy flesh. Lowering his head, he suckled one aroused tip.

Her reaction was reflexive, primal. She arched her back against the bed, gripping the sheets in her hands, inhaling deeply through clenched teeth. Dragging one leg slowly upward against his thigh, she pulled him close, cradling him in the softness of her body.

Storm unhooked the clasp of her slacks. The zipper rasped as he tugged it open. Snagging his thumbs around the waistband, he lowered her slacks over her hips. The matching strip of black lace panties soon followed. Her cowboy boots proved a challenge. Impatiently he raised himself from the bed to tug one, then the other off her feet. Finally she wore nothing—but a locket around her neck and a demure, almost uncertain look on her face.

Biting anxiously on her lower lip, she watched as he undressed in front of her. When he stepped out of his jeans, she caught her breath, her eyes widening—with second thoughts, or simple appreciation, he wasn't sure which.

His fears were put to rest, however, when they melded into a steamy embrace as he rejoined her on the bed. Their hands impatiently explored each and every inch of their bodies, leaving no secrets. He marveled at the firm tautness of her breasts, the flatness of her stomach, the softness of her skin. Lowering his hand past the mound of dark curls, he found her warm to his touch, moist as he tested her readiness.

It took only a moment to reach for and use protection. But she tensed when he fitted himself between her thighs, forcing him to hesitate. Brushing the hair from his face, he saw the uncertainty in her eyes. "Jasmine? What's wrong?"

"Nothing's wrong. It's just…I want our first time to be special. I don't want to disappoint you."

"Disappoint me?" He frowned and started to pull away. "Jasmine, how can you think I'd be disappointed?"

"Never mind," she said, shaking her head. Before he could reconsider, she clasped her hands around his narrow waist and raised her hips off the bed, silently urging him to finish what they'd started.

Knowing he was lost, Storm released a ragged breath and eased himself inside her, penetrating the last of her resistance.

And heard her soft gasp of pain.

He froze, holding himself still. His frown returning, he looked down at her, searching her face. Swearing softly beneath his breath, he already knew the answer to his question. Now he understood her hesitancy. He hadn't realized that he was her first.

Overwhelmed by the ramifications of what was happening, he whispered, "Jasmine, I can't. We shouldn't—"

"No," she said, her voice an urgent whisper. She held him tight, refusing to let him go. "It's what I want. I need you, Storm."

Unable to fight the power of both of their desires, Storm closed his eyes and gave in to his own wants. He plunged himself the rest of the way into her tight, virgin flesh.

Jasmine's body quivered beneath him. A flush of heat spread across her skin. She wrapped her legs around his hips and clung to him desperately.

He moved inside her cautiously. Her body gloved his, adjusting to the new demands. His heart pounded in his chest as his own need grew. Mindful of his responsibilities, he checked his urgency and brought them both slowly, carefully, to the edge. Then, when she was ready, with sharp, quick strokes he carried them to the point of no return.

She shuddered at the moment of climax, closing her eyes and crying out her pleasure. He followed her over the crest, finding release in her warm, giving body.

When it was over, he held her in his arms until her breath returned to normal and her heart slowed its rapid beat. Then, releasing her, he rolled over onto his side and sat on the edge of the bed. Dropping his elbows to his knees, covering his face with his hands, he allowed the guilt to flow over him.

He'd acted without thinking.

For a stolen moment he'd found solace in her sweet body.

But for the rest of his life he would have to live with the knowledge that he'd taken advantage of Jasmine at a time when she needed him most.

At his withdrawal, a chill settled over her. For the first time in her life Jasmine allowed her insecurities to get the better of her. Without thought of her inexperience, she'd given of herself. He'd told her that he was a man of many, many experiences. It wasn't any wonder that she'd disappointed him.

Her body warmed with the heat of embarrassment. Unable to face him, she clambered off the bed and hurried for the bathroom. Closing the door behind her, she came face-to-face with the evidence of her own folly. In the mirror, she stared at her too bright eyes, the pupils dilated with lingering excitement. Her lips were red and swollen from his caresses, as were her breasts. In the most private of places, she still throbbed with wanting him.

Choking back a sob, she turned from the mirror and wrenched the faucet on. The water drummed against the porcelain sink, masking the sound of her tears. Her hands shaking, she splashed water on her face and tried to control her runaway emotions. Grabbing a cloth from the towel rack, she washed away the evidence of their lovemaking.

It wasn't until she turned off the water that she realized she hadn't brought any clothes with her. The thought of facing him naked and exposed nearly overwhelmed her. Knowing she couldn't hide from him indefinitely, she wrapped herself in a towel and stepped toward the door.

But she couldn't do it. Jasmine froze, her hand on the doorknob. She couldn't face him. Not now, not knowing just how much of herself she had revealed.

With her back against the door, she sank to the floor, clutching the towel around her breasts. Fresh tears spilled down her cheeks as she lowered her head to her knees and gave in to the unwanted show of weakness.

She wasn't sure how long she stayed there, sitting on the floor, feeling alone and miserable. It wasn't until she heard the knock on the door that she roused herself from the depths of self-deprecation.

"Jasmine?"

The sound of Storm's concerned voice almost proved to be her undoing. She didn't trust herself to speak.

He knocked again, harder this time. "Jasmine, open the door."

Her voice muffled with emotion, she said, "Go away, Storm. I need a moment."

"You've had more than a moment," he said with a tone of impatience. Thumping the door one last time, she heard the helpless sound of his sigh. "Jasmine, why didn't you tell me? If I'd known that you were a—" He stopped abruptly. Cursing softly, he said, "Jasmine, did I hurt you?"

Heat scorched her face. Jasmine bit her lip against a flood of new tears. She'd never felt so mortified, so ashamed, in her life. "No, Storm. You didn't hurt me. It's just… I need my clothes. Would you mind—"

"Of course not," he said, sounding relieved at being given something to do. She heard his footsteps move away from the door, then return seconds later. "Jasmine, I have your clothes. But you have to open the door to get them."

Weak from crying, she struggled to her feet. She took in a breath of courage, then opened the door, her hand shaking on the knob.

Storm stood in front of her, dressed only in his

faded jeans, an unreadable expression on his somber face. But his eyes told a different story. There was concern in their dark recesses. Assessingly, he took in the tears staining her cheeks, the embarrassed flush of her face, the fist that held the thin towel around her body. In his hands, he held her rumpled clothes.

Jasmine averted her eyes, unable to face him. With her gaze focused on the bathroom's linoleum floor, she held out her free hand for her discarded clothes. "May I have my clothes please?"

"Not until you talk to me."

Stunned, she looked up at him, dropping her hand to her side. "There's nothing more to discuss."

"Bull. I'm not letting you go. Not like this. You're upset, and we need to talk about it."

"Upset? Why would I be upset?" Jasmine noted that the rising pitch of her voice only gave credence to his observation. But she couldn't stop the agitated flow of words. "First my mother confesses to a crime I had no clue she'd committed. Then I go to bed with the man whose brother she killed." She gave a hollow laugh, knowing she sounded on the verge of completely losing control. "It's just been one of those days, Storm."

Silence strained between them.

Then, quietly, he said, "It isn't like you to be bitter, Jasmine."

"I'm not bitter, Storm. I'm just being honest. This wasn't one of my finer examples of good judgment.

But don't worry, I'm not blaming you for what happened. We both got..." She swallowed hard, struggling to hold on to what was left of her pride. "...carried away. We simply made a mistake."

"Is that what you think it was? A mistake?"

The coolness of his tone sent a shiver down her spine. She considered sidestepping him, pushing past him to freedom. But along with her clothes, he held all the cards in this game of truth or dare. He had strength and size on his side.

"What do you want me to say, Storm? That it was my fault I didn't tell you the truth? You didn't know it was my—" Her voice broke. She hesitated, looking down at her bare toes before saying, "My first time. I don't blame you for being disappointed. I'm sure you were expecting so much more."

"That's what this is all about?" He sounded incredulous. "You think I'm disappointed?"

She lifted her trembling chin in a stubborn show of pride, but remained silent, not trusting herself to answer.

"Aw, Jasmine," he said, shaking his head. Before she could react, with a quickness that took her breath away, he reached out, linked his hand with hers and tugged her into the bedroom. Capturing her waist with his free hand, he pulled her close, holding her snug against him.

Startled, she clung tightly to the ends of the towel, looking up to see the steely determination in his eyes.

"You're wrong, Jasmine. What happened between us...it wasn't a disappointment. It was special, more than I could ever explain. But you are right about one thing, though. I didn't know it was your first time. Not until it was too late. If I had..." He left the thought unfinished, letting her imagination run wild. Sighing, he said, "If I gave you the wrong impression, then I'm sorry. But what I felt wasn't disappointment, it was guilt. I took advantage of you at a time when you needed comfort. I didn't deserve to be the first. I didn't deserve the gift you gave me."

Blinking in surprise, she searched his face for the truth—and found nothing but sincerity mixed with remorse hidden in his eyes. Unable to stop herself, she lifted a hand and smoothed a wayward strand of hair from his face, tucking it gently behind his ear. Letting her hand linger against his neck, she felt his strong pulse beneath her fingers.

Looking him straight in the eye, she whispered, "You're wrong, Storm. What I said before, about making a mistake, it wasn't true. You're the one I've waited for. The only one I've ever dreamed of being with. Don't you see? We were meant to be together. You have nothing to feel guilty about."

He lowered his head, pressing his forehead against hers. "I won't make any promises that I can't keep, Jasmine. Too much has happened. I don't know what the future holds for us."

She closed her eyes against the sting of disappointment. Fate might have brought them together, but it was working to keep them apart, as well. Struggling for control, she lifted her head and looked into his eyes. Her voice a whisper, she said, "I've never asked for a commitment. I only want what you can give me. Even if it's only a single night in your arms."

He stared at her, letting the silence gather between them. His dark-eyed gaze sent a trembling of awareness through her body. She held her breath and waited for him to answer.

Finally he nodded and said, "I can give you tonight."

For now, she told herself, that would have to be enough.

Twining her fingers through his hair, she tugged him close. She settled her lips upon his and felt the tension flow from her muscles. A new rush of desire billowed inside her as she let go of the pain of uncertainty in her heart, refusing to give in to her doubts. She gasped when Storm lifted her from her feet, cradling her in his arms.

As he carried her back to the bed, she told herself for now she felt safe and wanted.

Tomorrow would be soon enough for second thoughts.

Instead of the darkness and gloom she had expected, tomorrow greeted her with sunshine and brightness. As the early morning light seeped in through the cracks in the curtains, the sound of quiet, careful movements roused Jasmine from a sound sleep. Lazily she stretched a hand across the bed and discovered it empty.

Slowly opening her eyes, she blinked away the sandy grit of sleeplessness, feeling understandably tired and groggy. She hadn't slept much the night before. Too intent on making the most of each precious second of their stolen time together, both she and Storm had found little time to rest.

She sat up in bed and switched on the nightstand's lamp. Her breath caught at the unexpected sight that met her eyes.

Fully dressed in a pair of khaki pants and a long-sleeved, buttoned-down shirt, his hair still wet from a recent shower, Storm was in the midst of packing a suitcase. He stopped what he was doing and glanced over at her, his gaze wary.

"You're packing," she said needlessly.

"There's nothing more for me here." His voice sounded cold, emotionless. He picked up a shirt and slammed it into the case. "I've finished what I came to do. It's time for me to go back to New Mexico."

Pain zigzagged through her heart. She inhaled a sharp breath. "I see."

Stopping midreach for another shirt, he studied her, as though sensing her disappointment. He made his way to the bed. The mattress sank beneath his weight as he sat beside her.

Jasmine struggled to hide the tremors of apprehension that shook her body. The night she'd just spent wrapped in his arms seemed like a distant, almost forgotten dream. The ecstasy and fulfillment they'd shared seemed like nothing more than a broken memory.

Though she longed for his touch, he rested his elbows against his knees and kept his hands clasped firmly together. "Jasmine, I told you last night I couldn't make any promises."

"I know," she said, her trembling voice doing little to ease the anxious look from his face.

His frown deepened. "Too much has happened between us. Your mother, what she did to Raven—" His voice caught and he stopped, staring down at his fisted hands.

Jasmine swallowed at the growing lump of disbelief that had lodged in her throat. She felt the sting of tears and blinked hard, refusing to give in to the lure of vulnerability. Now was not the time for weakness. She must be strong. She must face the future. Even if that future promised only loneliness and heartache.

He took a breath, releasing it on a sigh. "There's just too much to forget, too many obstacles to overcome. We would never be able to put everything that's happened behind us. It would always stand in our way."

Not we, Jasmine answered silently. You, Storm. You are the only one who cannot forget.

Jasmine knew without question that if the roles were reversed and Storm's brother had been the one to hurt her family, she would find a way to forgive him. She would not allow a mistake from the past, something that he had no control over, to ruin their chance at happiness. She would do whatever it took for them to be together.

But she wasn't Storm.

She hadn't lived a life void of love and security.

Her family had cared deeply for her. They'd built her life on a foundation of concern and confidence. Unlike Storm, she'd never experienced the pain of being alone and unwanted.

Jasmine looked at him, her resolve melting as she saw the uncertainty that lined his face. His eyes moved restlessly, unable to meet her gaze. While the words he spoke were cold and flat, she knew there was a firestorm of emotion burning in his heart.

But it was hopeless. For thirty years Storm had survived by avoiding the very thing she longed to share with him—a close and loving relationship. She would not try to change his mind. No matter how much she wanted it to be different, she wouldn't beg him to stay.

Instead she stroked the powerful lines of his face. "It's all right, Storm. I understand."

He lifted his eyes, his gaze hesitant.

She smiled, despite the pain tearing her heart in two. "We'll always have last night. Just don't forget what we shared."

"That would be impossible," he said, giving her an uneasy smile.

She unclasped the compass from around her neck, the one her mother had given her. Taking his hand in hers, she placed the gold-plated compass on his palm and closed his fingers around it. At his questioning look, she said, "I want you to keep this, in case you ever need to find your way back to me. The compass will guide you, so you won't get lost."

With a sigh, he brushed his fingers through her hair, then cupped her chin in his hand. For a moment he stared at her, letting the regret shimmer in his eyes. Then, with a tenderness she would forever cherish, he bid her one last good-bye with a kiss.

Twelve

Two hours later, Storm approached the outskirts of town on Highway 191, heading for the airport in Bozeman. He'd left early, giving himself more than enough time to catch his four o'clock flight to Albuquerque. He saw no reason in prolonging his stay in Whitehorn.

He'd had his fill of the bad memories the town held for him.

Storm frowned. Not all the memories were bad, he admitted. Absently, he touched the breast pocket of his shirt, feeling the outline of the compass Jasmine had given him. Some were just destined to remain bittersweet.

He reached inside his pocket and fished out the compass. Holding it by its chain, he watched as the antique gold caught the sunlight, sending sparkles throughout the interior of the car.

He hadn't wanted to accept Jasmine's gift.

He'd wanted to push her and everything that reminded him of the time they'd spent together out of his mind. Coming to Whitehorn and searching for the truth behind his brother's death, had been one of the hardest tasks he'd ever had to face. Meeting Jasmine and losing his heart had only complicated matters.

Though he'd succeeded in finding his brother's murderer, once again he'd lost at love.

Closing his hand around its cool metal casing, he gripped the compass tightly. Despite her gift and her stoic show of pride, he knew Jasmine had been hurt by all that had happened.

Even worse, he knew that he'd been the cause of that pain.

Because of him and his relentless pursuit of the past, Jasmine had lost her mother, her innocence and her reason to hope. In less than two hours Celeste Monroe would be arraigned on the charges of murdering his brother. Instead of staying and facing what he'd wrought, once again he'd run away, unable to witness the final tableau.

He felt like the worst kind of coward.

His mood plummeting, he tucked the compass back into his pocket, telling himself he had no reason to feel guilty. He wasn't the one who'd pulled the trigger and taken a life. No, his crime was much more subtle. He'd come seeking revenge on the Kincaid family. And revenge he'd found....

He'd shattered their peaceful little family.

So why didn't he feel vindicated? Why did it feel as though he'd destroyed his last chance at a normal life?

Fighting the rising tide of bitterness, he told himself

Jasmine was better off without him. He'd been on his own for too many years. Even if he wanted to, he wouldn't know how to care for someone the right way. He'd only end up hurting her more if he stayed and tried to make a life with her.

Thump. The loud noise came from out of nowhere, startling him. Something large and dark had hit the windshield. Storm slammed on his brakes, swerving reflexively from danger and sending the car careering into the oncoming lane of traffic. Thankfully, the highway was deserted. No other car was in sight.

His heart pounding, he corrected his mistake and guided the car back into the right lane. The experience had left him shaken, not sure if he could drive. Besides, he needed to pull over to the side of the road to check for damage.

His tires whipped up a cloud of dust as he lurched to an unsteady stop. Shifting the gear into park, he tore open the door and stumbled out of the front seat. Relief settled over him at the feel of solid ground beneath his feet. Feeling as though he'd just sprinted five miles, he struggled for a breath and stared at the cracked windshield.

The morning air wafted over his flushed skin, cooling his agitated senses. Out of nowhere, an object had appeared and had smashed the windshield of his rented car. The safety glass had splintered, but held in place. There'd been no cars in front or behind him. Nothing that could have kicked up a loose rock from beneath its tires. Storm frowned. The impact had been too strong for just a pebble. It had to have been something large and heavy.

A flap of wings caught his attention.

Storm tore his stunned gaze from the windshield and squinted up into the sun-drenched sky. Soaring up above him was a large, dark bird. A raven.

Goose bumps prickled his skin, raising the hairs on the back of his neck. His mind was spinning with confusion. He glanced back at the damaged car and saw for the first time a single black feather lodged beneath the windshield wipers.

''Impossible,'' he murmured, feeling dazed as he reached for the unbroken feather.

Running his fingers over the soft, downy tufts, he considered the possibility. He'd been traveling close to sixty miles per hour. If a bird had hit the windshield at that speed, it never would have survived the impact.

But if it wasn't the bird, then what was it?

''Forget it,'' he said through clenched teeth, his voice lost on the wind that swept the empty expanse of road. ''It doesn't matter if it was a rock, a boulder or a house that landed on the car. The car's insured. It's not a problem.''

Still clutching the black feather, Storm slung himself into the front seat. He slammed the door too hard, causing the rearview mirror to vibrate, pushing his nerves even further on edge. Rocks and dirt spewed from the tires as he swung back onto the highway.

Tossing the feather to the seat beside him, he concentrated on the road ahead. The speedometer trembled as he pushed down on the accelerator. Fifty… sixty…seventy miles an hour and still climbing. No matter how much it felt like it, he refused to admit that he was running away.

The miles sped past in a blur. The wind ruffled his hair as it streamed in through the open window. Storm stole a wary glance at the feather. If he were a practicing, traditional Cheyenne, he'd say he'd been given a sign from the spirits. That his brother Raven was trying to communicate with him from the afterworld.

The morbid thought sent a shiver down his spine.

Even if he believed in the mystical powers of the spirits, which he didn't, what sort of message would they be trying to send him? That he was driving too fast? Or that he'd taken the wrong road?

Or maybe that he shouldn't be leaving, after all?

Stunned by the thought, Storm eased his foot off the pedal, slowing the car. If it was Raven trying to communicate with him, then why wouldn't he want him to leave Whitehorn? Raven, of all people, should know the heartache that the town represented. Surely he wouldn't want Storm to prolong his suffering.

Or could it be that he'd left unfinished business behind him? Storm admitted he'd left in a rush, leaving too many loose ends. First, there were Raven's remains. Once they were released from the coroner's office, he'd have to call and leave word on a proper burial. And there was Summer. He never did have a chance to tell his niece good-bye. Once again, he was abandoning the only living link to his brother.

Even more importantly, there was Jasmine.

The heavy hand of guilt pressed against his heart. As his brother had done before him, he'd allowed the Kincaid family to keep him from the woman he loved. Unlike Raven, however, it was his pride, not his courage that had finally defeated him.

Raven had stood up to Jeremiah Kincaid. He'd lost his life defending his right to be with Blanche. Storm had given up Jasmine without even a fight.

It wasn't any wonder he felt so guilty.

He couldn't leave, he realized, not like this.

Setting his jaw in a hard line of determination, Storm checked his mirrors for traffic. Assuring himself that both lanes were empty, he made a quick U-turn and headed back to Whitehorn.

"We're terribly sorry about the cancellation," Gladys Humphrey said, her round cheeks flushing with discomfort. Her hands fluttered to her throat as she gave a nervous laugh. "Our daughter insists that we come a few days early to visit her in California. Family...I'm sure you must understand."

Her husband remained noticeably silent. An impatient frown creasing his bulldog face.

"Yes, Mrs. Humphrey. I understand," Jasmine said softly. Her hand felt as heavy as lead as she handed Mrs. Humphrey the credit card receipt for their visit.

Without another word, the pair turned from the front desk and hurried for the exit. She watched as they stepped outside into the cool morning sunlight, leaving the door open behind them. Once they were out of sight, Jasmine let her shoulders slump in defeat, feeling too tired and drained of energy to even get up and shut the door herself.

In the past hour, two other guests had checked out early, unexpectedly canceling the rest of their stay at the Big Sky Bed & Breakfast. While their excuses were inventive, as well as polite, Jasmine knew the truth.

No one wanted to stay in the house of a confessed murderer.

Out of habit, Jasmine reached for the reassuring weight of the compass around her neck, and felt nothing but smooth, unadorned skin. She inhaled a quick breath as the memory of giving Storm the compass flashed in her mind.

Though it had been only a few hours since she'd last seen him, it seemed like a lifetime ago.

After her night away from the B and B, since returning home, she'd been in a rush, hurrying to catch up on neglected chores. After a quick shower and change, she'd made breakfast for their guests. Now, with the house almost empty, it was time to prepare herself for another ordeal. Her mother's arraignment.

"Did they leave?"

Aunt Yvette's quiet voice startled her. Jasmine glanced up to meet her aunt's crestfallen face. With a sigh, she nodded. "That's the last of them. The Humphreys, the Sterlings…they've all checked out, canceling the rest of their stay."

Yvette clucked her tongue in disapproval. "I don't know how to tell your mother. She's going to be so upset. Running the B and B has always been her pride and joy."

"Then we won't tell her that people are canceling their reservations. She's fragile enough, Yvette. I don't know if she can handle any more bad news."

"I don't know if I can handle any more bad news, either." Tears glistened in Yvette's eyes. She attempted a smile, and failed.

Jasmine covered her aunt's hand with hers, squeezing it gently. Good sign, or bad, they hadn't heard from her mother or the sheriff's office this morning. According to Yvette, no one had called the night before, either. Even David, their source of information, had been unusually quiet since her mother's confession. Not knowing what was happening seemed to make everything that much worse.

When Jasmine had returned this morning, Yvette hadn't questioned her absence. Though from the troubled look in her eyes, Jasmine knew Yvette had a good idea where, and with whom, she'd spent the night. However, she was grateful for her aunt's discretion. Storm's unexpected departure had been devastating enough. The last thing she needed was to face one of her family's well-intended inquisitions.

From the doorway, the sound of a car coming fast down the gravel lane caught her attention. Jasmine frowned, glancing impatiently at her wristwatch. It was getting late. They'd have to be leaving soon for the courthouse. Now wasn't the time for a visitor.

Yvette stepped toward the large front window. Her brow furrowed into a worried frown as she stared outside. "Jasmine, I—" She hesitated, uncertainty shadowing her voice. She looked at her niece. "I think you'd better come here."

The urgency of her aunt's request sent shivers of trepidation down Jasmine's spine. She rose on unsteady feet and crossed the room to the window. Glancing outside, she blinked in surprise, unable to believe her own eyes.

Traveling at a quick clip, Storm's silver-gray luxury car was approaching the B and B.

"Were you expecting Mr. Hunter?" Yvette asked, searching Jasmine's face for her reaction.

Jasmine shook her head, feeling numb. When they'd parted hours earlier, she hadn't planned to see Storm ever again. He'd made his intentions perfectly clear. He was leaving Whitehorn and her, and he wasn't looking back.

She had no idea why he'd returned now.

The car skidded to a stop in front of the B and B. Not waiting for the dust to settle, Storm stepped out onto the white rock drive. He seemed oblivious to the fine coating of grit powdering his navy blazer. He stood with his hands on his slender hips, staring up at the house. With his hair slicked back from his face, and his chiseled jaw set in a determined line, he looked every bit as formidable and as devastatingly handsome as she'd remembered.

Her tummy fluttered. She tried not to let her hopes get too high. But his coming here…it was a good sign, wasn't it? Perhaps he'd changed his mind, after all. Given a little time, maybe he'd decided he could live with everything that had happened between their families. Would it be too much to hope that he was finally ready to let go of the past?

Not waiting for him to seek her out, she turned from the window and hurried out the door. It wasn't until she stepped closer and saw his somber face that she slowed her step. Her heart thumped painfully against her chest. Instinctively she knew that whatever he'd come to tell her, it wasn't the happy ending she'd hoped for.

Not trusting her own willpower, she left a safe distance between them. Feigning a casual tone, she said, "I thought you had left."

"I did." His deep voice echoed in her ears. His

eyes never leaving hers, he said, "But there's something I forgot."

She licked her lips, her throat suddenly dry. "What was that?"

"You."

His blunt answer rocked her. The ground shifted beneath her feet. Her world felt as though it were spinning out of control. Reflexively she flinched when he stepped toward her.

He stopped, looked at her, seeming confused by her reaction.

Jasmine took a steadying breath. "I—I don't understand."

"There's nothing to understand. I'm not leaving Whitehorn, not without you."

She shook her head. "You can't be serious. I can't just…leave."

"Yes, you can, Jasmine." His voice rang with determination. "I want you to go upstairs and pack a bag. There's a four o'clock flight to Albuquerque. We can both be on that plane."

"You want me to leave Whitehorn," she said, still trying to make sense of the words. "Now? But what about my mother? The arraignment? How could I possibly leave her at a time like this?"

"There's no reason to stay, Jasmine," he said, his tone urgent. "We've both been hurt by what's happened. It's time for a fresh start. I love you, Jasmine. I want us to make that new start together."

"Oh, Storm," Jasmine said, her voice breaking under the weight of strained emotion.

She of all people knew just how difficult his coming here must have been. In a show of trust, Storm had finally put his fears behind him. He'd taken that giant first step toward making a commitment. He'd admitted just how much he cared.

If only it wasn't too little, too late.

"I love you, too, Storm. But I can't leave," she said, looking at him with all the regret she felt in her heart. "Not now, not like this. Not when my mother needs me."

Pain flickered in his eyes before a stony mask of indifference slipped into place. "She lied to you, Jasmine."

"Not on purpose. She made a mistake, Storm. I can't abandon her. Surely you can understand that."

He didn't answer. From the hard expression on his face, Jasmine knew he hadn't a clue what she was talking about.

Anger and frustration rose up inside her. Nothing had changed, not really. Just as before, Storm wouldn't allow his emotions to interfere in his life. When his own family had disappointed him all those years ago, instead of trying to help them, to change the fate they'd been handed, he'd abandoned them. He had run away and hadn't looked back.

Now he wanted her to do the same.

"Maybe you can't understand, after all," she said,

suddenly too tired to argue. "You've always seen things in black and white, haven't you? You've never been able to forgive and forget, even the smallest of mistakes. But I can."

Her voice broke. Tears blurred her vision. She swallowed hard, struggling to find the strength to finish what must be said. "I'm sorry, Storm. But I can't go with you to Albuquerque. My home is here in Whitehorn. I wish you could understand. My mother needs me. I won't abandon her. Not now, not ever."

With that, she turned her back on him. Striding to the front porch, she climbed the stairs, taking them two at a time, hurrying to put a safe distance between them. But in her heart she knew she would never be able to outrun the memory of his confused, pain-lined face.

Thirteen

The courthouse was unusually crowded.

Throngs of spectators milled in the halls, waiting for the show to begin. Despite the short notice, Jasmine wasn't surprised by the large turnout of local citizens. Whitehorn was a small town. Bad news traveled fast.

Besides, her mother had a reputation as an oddball. It wasn't any wonder that her latest example of eccentric behavior had drawn curiosity seekers. And, thanks to Jasmine's late uncle, Jeremiah Kincaid, and his ability to stir up trouble, people around these parts would travel far and wide to see what further trouble he could wreak, even from the grave.

A sudden hush fell across the courthouse as Jasmine made her way through the crowd. Bystanders scattered, making room for her, staring as she passed. Keeping her eyes focused straight ahead and her head held high, Jasmine was determined to not let the people of Whitehorn see the devastating effect her mother's murder confession had had upon her. No matter what the cost to her pride, she was here to support her mother.

Even if it meant losing everything she held dear—including the man she loved.

Jasmine strode to the front of the room, anxious to join her family. Aunt Yvette and Uncle Edward scooted over, making room for her in the first row behind the defendant's table.

Cleo leaned forward from her seat in the second row. "You're late," she whispered.

"I couldn't help it," Jasmine said, grimacing. "The parking lot was full. I had to park the Jeep a block past the movie theater and walk the rest of the way. Have I missed anything?"

Cleo shook her head. "Nothing's happened yet. There's been a delay."

"A delay?" Jasmine frowned, her stomach churning with unease. "What sort of delay?"

"They won't tell us," Yvette chimed in, keeping her voice hushed. "All I know is that Ross Garrison, the attorney we hired for Celeste, came out and told us there was a meeting going on in the judge's chambers. And that as soon as he heard anything, he'd let us know."

"Is that good news or bad?" Jasmine asked, her frown deepening.

Yvette shrugged. "It's anyone's guess."

The tall, silver-haired figure of Garrett Kincaid caught her eye. Ignoring the curious stares of the crowd, he strode toward Jasmine and her family. Resting one hand on the back of her seat, Garrett leaned forward and whispered, "Something's going on. The sheriff and his deputies were out at the ranch house last night. They spent the whole night searching my study. Made a damn mess, too." He grunted his dissatisfaction. "Even tore a hole in the wall behind my desk."

"Did they say anything?" Jasmine asked, trying not to let her anxiety show through.

"Not to me they didn't," he said, giving his head an impatient shake. "But I'd never seen such a bunch of grim faces. If you ask me, things weren't going as smooth as the sheriff had planned." Frowning, he glanced around the crowded room. "Well, I'd better be going if I want to find a seat. You tell your mama that if there's anything I can do, she should just call."

Jasmine gave a polite smile, but didn't answer. At the moment there was nothing any of them could do. Her mother had confessed to the crime of murder. It would be in the hands of the court to decide her fate.

The minutes passed excruciatingly slowly. The din of excited voices reverberated through the courtroom, echoing off of the walls. The noise gave Jasmine a pounding headache, making the ordeal even more discomfiting. When a sudden hush fell across the room, she wasn't sure whether to be relieved or even more worried.

Something, or someone, had gotten the crowd's attention.

The buzz of voices resumed, only louder this time.

Though she was dying of curiosity, Jasmine refused to turn around to look to see who, other than her mother, could be causing such a stir in the crowd. Which is why she jumped in her seat when someone tapped her shoulder.

Jasmine whirled to face the newcomer. Her breath caught in her throat, her eyes widened in surprise as she stared up into Storm's hesitant face.

"If it isn't too late," he said, loud enough for those around them to hear, "I'd like to sit beside you during your mother's arraignment."

Her mouth opened to answer, but the words of acceptance wouldn't form. For a heart-stuttering moment Jasmine couldn't answer. She was still too stunned by his unexpected appearance to speak.

Her heart racing, she tried to make sense of it all. Instead of leaving town, Storm had stayed. He was here, in the courthouse, wanting to join her at a time when she needed him most. The implication of his change of heart was obvious.

He was telling her in his own way that he was ready to forgive and forget the past.

He was ready to stand beside her, and her family, no matter what the outcome of today's arraignment.

Tears of relief prickled her eyes. Biting her lip to stop the maudlin show of emotion, Jasmine nodded and scooted over to make room for Storm beside her on the bench.

It was a tight fit. Jasmine had to tuck her arm beneath Storm's wide shoulder. The rest of their bodies—hips, thighs, and legs—were pressed together, not an inch of space to spare. But she didn't mind. She savored the warm, secure feel of his body next to hers.

With an audible sigh of relief, Storm picked up her hand in his, linking his fingers with hers. No other words were necessary. His supportive actions spoke volumes to her, and to those around them.

If it wasn't for her mother's impending arraignment, Jasmine had never felt happier or more contented. If she hadn't been certain of the future before, she was sure now. Despite the obstacles standing between them, Storm had found his way back to her. He'd proven to her that he was her soul mate, her one true love. In her heart, she had always known they were destined to be together.

Once again, a hush fell across the room.

This time her mother's appearance in the courtroom had caused the reaction. Dressed in a pale, peach-colored tunic and matching pants, Celeste looked tired and frail. Without makeup, the dark circles beneath her eyes were even more obvious. Her hair, normally so carefully styled, hung limp and unkempt around her face. She wore a confused, almost dazed look.

Jasmine's heart lurched at Celeste's disheveled appearance. She stood, reaching out to her mother. But before she could murmur a word of reassurance, the

Blue River County district attorney, followed closely by the presiding judge, entered the courtroom. The bailiff called out the opening of the session, warning the crowd to stand and be silent.

Obligingly the crowd grew quiet. Only the shifting of feet as the crowd stood sounded in the room.

Taking his seat at the bench, the judge picked up his gavel and rapped it sharply. "Be seated." Over the noise of settling bodies, he narrowed an impatient glance at the district attorney. "Mr. Corwin, do you have a motion for me?"

Clearing his throat, the D.A. rose to his feet. "Yes, Your Honor. If it pleases the court, the state requests that all charges against Celeste Kincaid Monroe be dropped."

A roar of astonishment swept the courtroom.

Jasmine's heart leaped in her chest. Her shocked gaze traveled from her mother's confused face to Storm's startled look. Everyone seemed surprised by the turn of events.

The judge rapped his gavel, once, twice, three times before the uproar subsided. His expression stern, he said, "Motion granted. All charges are dropped. The case is dismissed."

After a final tap of his gavel, the judge stood and left the courtroom, disappearing through his chamber doors. With his departure, all hell broke loose throughout the courtroom. From the four corners of the room, the crowd speculated with various degrees of surprise and outrage on this unexpected turn of events.

Despite the confusion spinning in his own mind, Storm put a protective arm around Jasmine's shoulder, shielding her from the startled outburst of the crowd. He leaned close and said, "Do you have any idea what's happening?"

She shook her head. "No, I haven't a clue. I'm just as much in the dark as you are."

Sheriff Rawlings, accompanied by Detective Gretchen Neal, approached the defense table. Spotting Storm and Jasmine's family in the crowd, he motioned for them to join him. Pointing to a side door, he said, "I think it'd be better if we waited out the crowd in one of the conference rooms." He nodded at Storm. "It'll give me a chance to explain the situation to you, Mr. Hunter. As well as to Mrs. Monroe's family."

Storm didn't bother to argue. Any protest would have been lost over the excited voices of the crowd. Instead, along with Jasmine and her family, Storm allowed himself to be shepherded into a nearby conference room.

The sudden stillness of the room felt as welcome as a cooling breath of relief. Looking exhausted, Celeste collapsed into a nearby chair. Yvette and Cleo took chairs on either side, flanking Celeste in a show of support. The rest of the family hovered nearby, leaving Storm to feel like an intruder in this private scene. Instead of joining her family, to his grateful relief, Jasmine remained beside him.

At the opposite end of the room, Sheriff Rawlings conferred with Gretchen Neal in a whispered conversation. The detective shook her head, her response too quiet to overhear. Then, with a quick nod, Sheriff Rawlings turned his attention to the small group. "I guess you must be wondering what's going on. Before I give you the details, I want to apologize for springing all of this on you on such short notice. If we'd been given more time, we would have informed you of the new developments in the case before the court appearance today."

"What new developments, Sheriff?" David Hannon demanded. He stood at the opposite end of the conference table, keeping a discreet distance from Storm.

The sheriff sighed, looking tired and worn out. "Yesterday, after hearing Mrs. Monroe's confession, Detective Neal and I went out to the ranch house to take another look at the crime scene."

Crime scene...Garrett's study at the ranch house. Jasmine glanced up at Storm. From the startled look in her eyes, Storm realized that for the first time she'd finally gotten the connection between the study and his odd behavior on the day they'd visited Garrett Kincaid. She now knew that he'd had one of his feelings during their visit, that he had sensed the study as being the place where Raven had died.

Storm met her gaze with a steady look of his own. Sensing her surprise, he reached a reassuring arm around her shoulders and pulled her close.

Giving Celeste an apologetic glance, Sheriff Rawlings said, "I'll be honest with you, Mrs. Monroe. Something about your confession just didn't ring true."

"But I told you everything just as it happened," Celeste said, shaking her head and looking confused.

"Just as you *thought* it had happened," Sheriff Rawlings said, his words firm, brooking no argument. "Let me tell you what we found. First of all, the gun you gave us didn't match the type of bullet that we'd found lodged in Raven Hunter's remains."

A murmur of surprise rose from the group.

Ignoring the reaction, the sheriff continued. "In the ranch house study, we examined the wall exactly opposite of where you told us that you stood on the night Raven Hunter died. After a little digging inside the wall we found the bullet that you'd fired. Also, hidden behind the wallboard, we found another gun. A gun that we believe to be the murder weapon." The sheriff glanced across the room, looking directly at Storm. "There was only one set of fingerprints on that gun. And they belonged to Jeremiah Kincaid."

Storm flinched at the news. Jasmine placed a hand on his arm, glancing up at him with a look of concern.

Then, just as quickly as it had taken hold, he felt the tension gripping his muscles slowly relax. Along with the truth finally came acceptance. Storm had always believed Jeremiah to be the murderer. That was why he'd been so shocked by Celeste's confession. Now, despite everything, he found comfort in the fact that he hadn't been wrong, after all.

Sheriff Rawlings heaved a sigh. "It's my and Detective Neal's opinion that, in the course of the fight between Jeremiah and Raven, Jeremiah used the distraction of his sister's entrance into the study as an opportunity to pull a gun from hiding and shoot Raven point-blank in the stomach. The trajectory of the bullet lodged in Raven's rib cage confirms this theory. Given the new evidence, we had no choice but to let Mrs. Monroe go free."

A stunned silence filled the room.

Then Cleo let out a whoop of disbelief, breaking the stillness. "That nasty old bastard. I only wish Jeremiah hadn't died so we could nail his ornery old hide to the wall."

"Cleo, really," Celeste said, a shocked look on her face. But the look quickly dissolved into a wan smile.

The ice had finally been broken. Hugs and congratulations were exchanged among Jasmine and her family.

Storm stood at the fringe of the group, feeling out of place, overwhelmed by what had just occurred. He'd been ready to support Jasmine and her family, no matter what might have happened. But the charges had been dropped, the mystery was solved, and all had been accomplished without the tragedy of tearing Jasmine's family apart.

The worst was over. Now all that was left was to wait to see if Jasmine's family would be able to accept him as a part of her life.

As though sensing his unease, Jasmine crossed the room to rejoin him. A slow smile lit her face as she wrapped her arms around his neck and pulled him close. "It's over, Storm," she whispered. "It's finally over."

Without waiting for a response, she stood on tiptoe and kissed him. A long, sultry kiss on the lips. A kiss that promised so much more to come.

Lost in Jasmine's embrace, Storm didn't notice Celeste's approach until he heard a discreet clearing of the throat. Abruptly he ended the kiss. Not quite as intimidated by the intrusion, keeping her arm anchored at his waist, Jasmine turned to face her mother.

Looking from her daughter to Storm, Celeste took a deep breath, then released it with a sigh. "First of all, I'd like to apologize to you, Storm. My behavior toward you since your return to Whitehorn has been abominable. I can only hope, under the circumstances, you understand why I felt the need to distance myself from you."

Storm opened his mouth to answer.

Celeste held up a quieting hand. "Before you say

anything, hear me out. At first I tried to convince Jasmine that you and she were ill-matched. With good reason, I might add. Not only is there a difference in your ages, but the history between our families seemed to be working at odds against the two of you. But now…'' Her voice broke. She swallowed hard as tears of remorse filled her eyes. ''Now, seeing the two of you together, I realize that standing between you and Jasmine is wrong. Just as it was wrong for Jeremiah to keep Blanche and Raven apart.''

Storm felt his heart catch with surprise. He'd never thought he would hear a Kincaid admit that she was wrong. Perhaps there was such a thing as a miracle, after all.

With a trembling smile Celeste said, ''My daughter is a very determined woman. She's told me that you are the man she's meant to be with. I believe her. So much so that I'd like to be the first to welcome you into our family…if you'll have us.''

For the first time in his life Storm felt the power of love. Despite the differences between them, Jasmine's mother was ready to forgive and forget, all for the sake of her daughter's happiness. He envied Jasmine and her family for the closeness they shared.

''I'd like that very much, Mrs. Monroe.'' He glanced at Jasmine, raising a questioning brow. ''That is, if Jasmine still wants me to be a part of her life.''

''Don't be silly.'' Jasmine laughed. ''Of course, I still want you in my life. I'd never given up hope,

Storm.'' A twinkle of mischief lit her eye. ''Why do you think I gave you my compass? I knew it would lead you back home, where you belonged.''

Home. The word had never sounded so good. It described perfectly the way he felt in his heart. It was as though, after a long and trying journey, he'd finally found his way home.

Home, in Jasmine's arms.

Epilogue

The crowd spilled out of the living room of the B and B and into the large front lobby. Unlike the grim courthouse scene of just two months earlier, this gathering was a celebration of new beginnings.

Today, Jasmine and Storm's wedding day, there were no unhappy endings allowed.

Jasmine had chosen a simple white dress for the occasion. It was a form-fitting style, with a flared hem that ended just above her knees and emphasized the slender curves of her body. In deference to the day, instead of her usual black cowboy boots, she wore a special pair of white ones. Hand-tooled, of course. In place of a veil, tiny sprigs of mountain wildflowers were pinned in her hair. Other than the gold-plated compass around her neck—the gift Storm had returned when he'd decided not to venture beyond Whitehorn's boundaries ever again—she wore no other jewelry. As of yet.

Jasmine frowned. Maybe she'd taken back the compass too soon, she mused as she searched the crowd for the wayward man of her dreams.

Storm was nowhere in sight.

By the living room fireplace, she spotted David and

Gretchen Neal, deep in a conversation with Cleo and Ethan Redford. Frannie and her husband, Austin Parker, sidled up to join the boisterous group. As Jasmine passed by, they raised their champagne glasses in a mock toast.

With a grin and a wave, she continued past, determined not to be deterred from her goal—finding Storm.

Her mother, Aunt Yvette and Uncle Edward were stationed at the front door, greeting their guests as they arrived. Celeste raised an eyebrow in question as Jasmine neared.

"Storm?" Jasmine mouthed in a silent question.

Celeste shrugged, looking beautiful and refreshed, more like her old self in a gauzy dusty-rose caftan.

Yvette pointed to the back of the house, toward the kitchen. "I think I saw him heading that way just a few minutes ago." A mischievous smile touched her face. "Actually, I believe it was more like he was led against his will. The group he was with looked very persuasive."

Jasmine sighed her impatience. Though she wasn't usually a stickler for punctuality, this was one ceremony she didn't want to be late for.

Her boots thumped against the wooden floor as she strode down the wide hall and made a beeline for a group of guests who were lingering in the corridor outside the kitchen. Among them she recognized a smiling Summer and Gavin Nighthawk. Garrett Kincaid stood next to Jackson Hawk and his wife, Maggie. In the center of the group, she finally spotted Storm.

He smiled when he saw her, looking much too handsome in his dark suit and starched-white shirt, making it hard to stay impatient with him. The whiteness of his shirt contrasted nicely with the coppery hue of his skin and his long, dark hair. His eyes twinkled with amusement at her exasperated expression.

Instead of irritation, a hot surge of longing thrummed through her veins. Jasmine sucked in a steadying breath, getting a grip on her runaway libido. Later, she told herself, there would be plenty of time to satisfy her more lustful needs.

For now there was a wedding that was about to begin without the bride and the groom.

She plunged through the group and found her way to his side. "Storm," she said, her calm voice belying the butterflies dancing in her stomach, "do you have any idea what time it is?"

"Funny you should ask," Jackson said, interrupting her demand. "We were just trying to convince Storm to adopt the more traditional ways of the Cheyenne. Unlike the Anglos, keeping an eye on the clock just isn't as important to our people. We follow a more natural time rhythm." He made a waving motion with his hand. "You know...go with the flow?"

"I'm sorry, Jackson. But time's important when you have fifty guests and a minister waiting for you," Jasmine countered, smiling through clenched teeth.

Maggie Hawk gave her husband's arm a playful

swat. "Don't listen to him, Jasmine. Jackson is the most impatient man I've ever met. He's more of a stickler for schedules than he'd ever own up to."

Jackson glowered at his wife before planting a loving kiss on the tip of her nose.

"Now, don't you be mad at Storm, Jasmine," Garrett Kincaid drawled. "If he got a little sidetracked, trust me, it wasn't his fault. We've just been discussing a little business with him."

"Business?" Today of all days? she added silently.

As though he'd read her mind, Storm reached out and pulled her into his arms. His breath tickled her ear as he whispered, "I didn't exactly have a choice."

Jackson slapped Storm on the back, a wide grin splitting his face. "Storm has just agreed to act as tribal counsel for us on the Laughing Horse Reservation."

Jasmine blinked in surprise. While they hadn't discussed future plans in detail, Storm had assured her that he had no intention of leaving Whitehorn and forcing her to choose between her family and him. She'd been grateful for his decision, but she'd wondered what he intended to do now that he had closed his law office in New Mexico.

Storm was watching her closely, measuring her for a reaction. Jasmine considered the possibility. The thought of him returning to his roots on the reservation warmed her heart. It was where he was born, where he belonged. It was another important step in his acceptance of the past.

She smiled up at him. "I think that it's a wonderful idea. Congratulations, Storm."

His smile of relief sent a shiver down her spine. He truly was a most amazing man. In the past two months he'd seemed to change in front of her very eyes. He was more open with his feelings. She'd noticed a gradual letting go of his inhibitions. When, as a wedding present, her mother had given them a parcel of land along Blue Mirror Lake to build a house, the last of his insecurities seemed to have vanished. She'd even caught him smiling, relaxing, truly enjoying himself in her family's company.

Yes, she told herself, her smile deepening, the future did indeed look bright.

"Don't you two take too long on that honeymoon," Garrett said, interrupting her thoughts. "We've got a lot of work to do to get this casino/resort back on the right track before winter sets in. Now that we've moved to the new site and gotten away from that stubborn vein of bedrock, the construction's moving along full-steam-ahead."

"The casino/resort's going to represent an unusual alliance between the whites and Native Americans," Jackson ventured.

"A lucrative one, I hope," Garrett added with a nod and a smile. "I predict that in the near future, Whitehorn's going to become quite a popular spot."

Jasmine sighed. "That's all well and good, gentlemen. But right now I've got more important things on my mind...like a wedding."

No sooner had she said the words than she heard the sound of her mother's voice directing their guests into the side parlor, where they'd set up chairs and a makeshift altar in front of the windows facing Blue Mirror Lake and the peaks of the Crazy Mountains.

The group broke apart, joining the milling crowd as they followed Celeste's instructions.

To her relief, Jasmine finally found herself alone with Storm. She looked up at him, feeling suddenly nervous. "It's been a short two months. Are you sure you're ready for this?"

"I couldn't be any more certain if I'd had two years," he said, his expression somber. "I want to marry you, Jasmine. I want to spend the rest of my life with you here in Whitehorn. Nothing will ever change my mind."

She breathed a sigh of relief. "That's all I needed to hear. I love you, too, Storm. I can't wait to be your wife."

Without another word, she leaned forward and settled her lips on his, sealing the promise with a kiss. Then, releasing him, she twined her fingers in his, holding his hand tightly as they made their way into the parlor, ready to face their future together.

* * * * *

SILHOUETTE®
SPECIAL EDITION™

AVAILABLE FROM 19TH JULY 2002

THE NOT-SO-SECRET BABY Diana Whitney

That's My Baby!

Before mum-to-be Susan Mitchell told Jarod Bodine about their baby she had to find out what sort of father he was—by tutoring his son. But Susan hadn't expected to fall in love with the recalcitrant boy...or his father!

BACHELOR COP FINALLY CAUGHT? Gina Wilkins

Hot Off the Press

Police Chief Dan Meadows had always thought of Lindsey Gray as a sister. So he couldn't understand why, all of a sudden, he was noticing her curves. He couldn't be falling for her...could he?

WHEN I DREAM OF YOU Laurie Paige

Windraven Legacy

For generations scandalous secrets had divided the rival families of Megan Windom and Kyle Herriot. So how could one dance sweep them into a treacherous whirlpool of primal forbidden desire?

DADDY TO BE DETERMINED Muriel Jensen

Who's the Daddy?

Independent woman Natalie Browning had given up on love—but *not* on motherhood. Then she met single father Ben Griffin, who was honourable, intelligent, and *incredibly sexy*...her perfect daddy candidate!

FROM THIS DAY FORWARD Christie Ridgway

Annie Smith had yet to fall in love and everywhere she turned she came face-to-face with sexy Griffin Chase. But how could the housekeeper's daughter get involved with the heir to the Chase fortune?

HOME AT LAST Laurie Campbell

Detective JD Ryder was the only man that could help Kirsten find her three missing children. But she'd shared a past with JD and still kept a very special secret!

0702/23a

AVAILABLE FROM 19TH JULY 2002

SILHOUETTE®
Sensation™

Passionate, dramatic, thrilling romances

HARD TO HANDLE Kylie Brant
A HERO IN HER EYES Marie Ferrarella
TAYLOR'S TEMPTATION Suzanne Brockmann
BORN OF PASSION Carla Cassidy
COPS AND...LOVERS? Linda Castillo
DANGEROUS ATTRACTION Susan Vaughan

Intrigue™

Danger, deception and suspense

THE MAN FROM TEXAS Rebecca York
THE HIDDEN YEARS Susan Kearney
SPECIAL ASSIGNMENT: BABY Debra Webb
COLORADO'S FINEST Sheryl Lynn

Superromance™

*Enjoy the drama, explore the emotions,
experience the relationship*

THE WRONG BROTHER Bonnie K Winn
THE COMMANDER Kay David
BIRTHRIGHT Judith Arnold
THE FAMILY WAY Rebecca Winters

Desire™

Two intense, sensual love stories in one volume

THE MILLIONAIRE'S FIRST LOVE
THE MILLIONAIRE COMES HOME Mary Lynn Baxter
THE BARONS OF TEXAS: KIT Fayrene Preston

SEDUCED BY THE SHEIKH
SLEEPING WITH THE SULTAN Alexandra Sellers
HIDE-AND-SHEIKH Gail Dayton

HER PERSONAL PROTECTOR
ROCKY AND THE SENATOR'S DAUGHTER Dixie Browning
NIGHT WIND'S WOMAN Sheri WhiteFeather

0702/23b

2 FREE

books and a surprise gift!

We would like to take this opportunity to thank you for reading this Silhouette® book by offering you the chance to take TWO more specially selected titles from the Special Edition™ series absolutely FREE! We're also making this offer to introduce you to the benefits of the Reader Service™—

- ★ FREE home delivery
- ★ FREE gifts and competitions
- ★ FREE monthly Newsletter
- ★ Exclusive Reader Service discount
- ★ Books available before they're in the shops

Accepting these FREE books and gift places you under no obligation to buy, you may cancel at any time, even after receiving your free shipment. Simply complete your details below and return the entire page to the address below. *You don't even need a stamp!*

YES! Please send me 2 free Special Edition books and a surprise gift. I understand that unless you hear from me, I will receive 4 superb new titles every month for just £2.85 each, postage and packing free. I am under no obligation to purchase any books and may cancel my subscription at any time. The free books and gift will be mine to keep in any case.

E2ZEA

Ms/Mrs/Miss/Mr ....Initials.......................

BLOCK CAPITALS PLEASE

Surname ....

Address ....

....

....Postcode..................

Send this whole page to:
UK: FREEPOST CN81, Croydon, CR9 3WZ
EIRE: PO Box 4546, Kilcock, County Kildare (stamp required)